HAN M GREENBARG

Scurts Flightplan

First edition

ISBN: 978-1-7325029-4-9

This book was professionally typeset on Reedsy.
Find out more at reedsy.com

Contents

1

Gummy Bear Grenades

Entry 1.

February 13th, Year 2035. 2:03 pm. Kill your demons, they said. They won't plague you ever again. Some demons don't like to stay dead. Sometimes one comes floating back up onto the front porch with a chocolate covered rifle and a basket of gummy bear grenades offering to make amends. If you knew what I was. If you only knew.

My forty-ninth birthday. Three months until I'm supposed to die according to Robbie Decker. If you look outside the airport windows you will see a naked city skyline. No state in the United States is recognizable. I hear that the rest of the world is worse off but what do I know? I flew commercial planes then bagged groceries until the machines took over and after that I got paid through any means possible. Creative thinking is not my strength...I know it was yours, Anna. You did enough hard thinking for the both of us. Everyone told me I was innocent. They said I didn't put you in the ground. Tell me. Am I a murderer? Do I deserve to die?

"My name is Damon R Scurto."

"And why are you here with us today?" Blintz Garfrinks asked me, his fingers rapidly shuffling a stack of extra thick cards.

"I did something bad."

"What did you do, Mr. Scurto?"

"I killed someone."

"Who did you kill?" they said in unison.

"The love of my life."

My friends at baggage claim keep me company when I'm at my most needy but it's never the same as a woman by my side. I have to put up with these nutty weirdos who are all older than I am and they don't even let me gripe about my ailments without bringing up their own.

I have no internet access so I type this in hopes of someone one day finding it on the hard drive if the darn machine hasn't melted in the aftermath of what's to come. I just started these entries after borrowing this laptop from Richberg. He's a 58-year-old man who likes to eat paper and shares my habit of pacing the terminal barefoot in his dress blues...I don't wear a uniform, I just wear the same frayed jeans and black t-shirt day after day. And the sweat odor is becoming rancid.

"Happy birthday," the bobby-bangs lady says out of the somber blue, slapping me on the back. "What'd you turn? Forty-five? Fifty-six?"

"Thanks, Lyrna. Forty-nine."

"Wowzy, you are cute for that age. Paunchy, huh? Beer, maybe the mashed taters, or you from like the other coast with like fried crabs and stuff?"

I came to this crackly nuthouse of my own will. Earlier today I walked into a police station and was greeted by a single officer behind a plastic shielded desk. I spoke through the microphone on the other side to get his attention.

"I'm here to confess a murder," I said to him.

He raised his head, looking half-asleep and bored for days. "Of who?"

"A woman named Anna Gard."

His eyes drooped further and he went back to scribbling on paper. A long growl came through the speaker on his end. I spoke again.

"Officer, I need to be locked up or something. I can't sleep with the guilt."

"Are you off your crazy meds, civilian?"

"I need to talk to someone." I tapped the window.

He glanced up. "Are you homeless?"

"Yeah. But that's not why I'm here."

"Have you applied for a state-run room?"

"It costs fifty bucks in this city. I don't work."

"I can send you to our local shelter. Helmut Richberg is the one you will talk to about staying in a room. And as for your confession, here is the number of the current available therapist in our district."

"Okay." I took the card that he flicked through the credit card size slot. "But I'm a criminal. I need to be locked up."

"Sure you do."

"Officer, please reconsider sending me back out there. I just came in here to protect you all from my deadly force."

The officer laughed then coughed extra loud. "Look, as long as you haven't harmed our government I can't arrest you. Was this woman a government official?"

"No."

"Then you are free to go. And by the way, Anna Gard's killer was caught years ago. Robbie Decker. He's no longer our problem or yours. Have a good day, civilian."

"My name's Damon," I said.

The officer didn't speak another word. No one else came into the station. So I followed his directions and ended up at the entrance of this airport. The name of it has been scratched off along with all signage inside. It took at least twelve knuckle-bruising knocks on the broken sliding doors before my first geezer friend Richberg arrived on the other side to let me in.

And that is how I got here, Anna. That's how I'm still alive in this self-destructing world of militia carpet bombers, power nabbing dark horses, and bloodthirsty state officials. Gonna be one hell of a midlife crisis. I wish you were here with me, baby.

2

Therapist

Entry 2.

February 14th, 4:45 pm. After fifteen minutes in her presence I kick off my boots and walk barefoot back and forth, tattered jean bottoms swiping the floor. Fiddle with my glasses the entire session, once every few minutes bringing them back to perch on my nose. I mumble your name a lot, Anna. And my therapist, sheesh. The way she looks at me pushes me too much. I have to think about your face, your soft brown passionate eyes, how you tilted your head down and to the side when I smiled at you. Therapist's name is Camille and all I really know of her so far is that she enjoys nursing a bottle of dry wine with each hour session. We meet on the third floor of the airport where all the gates are empty and there is nothing but glass windows for what seems like miles. Planes are sitting on the taxiway.

What follows is the conversation she recorded that day. She writes our sessions like a stage play...at least that's what it looks like on her sheets of paper. I don't think I talk as much as she would like.

Camille: Do you think you deserve punishment?

I don't even pause a beat.

Damon: I think I deserve justice.

Camille: What is your definition of justice, Mr. Scurto?

I see your face as I answer each question.

Damon: To see the grave of Anna Gard.

Camille: Are you a blood relative?

My breath is heavy. I wipe sweat from my neck down onto my shirt.

Damon: No, ma'am.

Camille: Husband?

I smirk before answering.

Damon: No, ma'am.

Camille: Then that trip cannot be allowed.

This woman is relentless. Very pretty and strong-headed. But relentless. Dammit I hate therapists.

Damon: I need to know that I did it, Camille.

Camille: That you are the murderer.

Damon: Yes.

Camille: Is that justice to you, Mr. Scurto?

Damon: Yes. Very much justice.

Camille: And what about her wishes?

I find myself almost crushing the frames of my glasses in my hand.

Damon: She's dead.

Camille: Can she not lay quietly?

Damon: Not until my conscience is cleared.

I watch her lean back in her chair, as she finally sets the bottle of wine on the floor.

Camille: Do you have any pictures?

Damon: Pictures?

Camille: Of Anna. On your phone, in your wallet?

Here's the thing, Anna. I love beautiful women but I also love to lie. It's fun. The reactions are funny. You'd think I'd have learned by now to be honest every second. Nope.

Damon: I don't have a wallet and my phone was stolen by a serial killer.

Camille: You are a trip, Mr. Scurto. How far do you think we will get if you lie?

Damon: How do I get rid of this guilt, Camille? If there is a pill, fine, I'll take that. I'll smoke something if I have to.

She looks at me with such cold vigor I swear she was there all those years ago watching me break your heart.

Camille: You swallow your ego before you come to me next time.

She slaps the pen down so hard it bounces.

"Next time, call me Damon."

3

Wrong Restaurant

Entry 3.

February 15th, 5:20 pm. He thinks my name is Ryder Brackett. I used a fake name when I called his phone number. The police department reluctantly gave me his number but I want to know all he knows about you, Anna. Any evidence helps. I don't know what is truth or lie, but he says he has something of yours. Your diary. He is paying for dinner at a diner ten blocks from the airport. He is your convicted killer, wrongly convicted in my opinion.

The government pardoned all criminals except ones who committed crimes against the state and the rest of them are free. The police do not come after anyone unless it is past curfew in the city. As long as we wear our civilian ID bracelets we can go into any public building. The rest of life here means special government permission for everything else.

On our first meeting Robbie Decker held out both hands formed to fists. "Sour candy or butterscotch drop. Pick one."

I looked his body up and down as he stared right at my face. He didn't look like a bad man. He was too willowy, too soft-complexioned.

"Why?"

His plastic-framed glasses slipped down his nose as I pushed my wire-rimmed specs back up.

"If you don't play my game, I don't play yours, Mr. Scurto."

"Crap," I said. "You know my real name already."

"I know a lot more than that, my friend. Thanks to your ex Anna. Or should I call her your dead heart in a jar?"

"Butterscotch drop."

He opened his right hand. "Nicely chosen. I prefer sour candy all day."

I glanced at the diner across the street. Two guards stood outside the door.

"Where is the diary?" I asked Robbie.

"Ah ah. Eat it first." He motioned to the candy drop in my hand. "Then we talk."

I've always assumed I could be friends with anyone as long as I smiled big and turned on the charm. My mom said I had a way of killing softly with my adorable green eyes and round face. But now, those same attributes seem to get me in trouble rather than get me what I want. Getting old and tubby doesn't help my case much. Plus the hair loss. And flecks of grey on what's left on the top of my head.

"Can you tell me why you said that I have three months to live...and telling me that over the phone?"

We had our wristbands scanned by the guards before gaining entry to the diner. It smelled like the epitome of salty fries and grilled burgers and appeared as though we were the only ones giving our business today.

"You don't just answer a call with the words 'yes this is Robbie, you have three months before you die.' You don't lead with that."

Robbie sat on the edge of the booth farthest from the door. "That was the polite version, Mr. Scurto. I pick my words carefully in the presence of a mentally unstable man."

I decided not to refute his insult. He was paying for my survival.

"It's on me, my friend," he said. "And you know why? You are the lowest of the low between the two of us. And living on borrowed time?" He hissed behind his teeth. "Must be rough."

"Thank you." My throat was so dry. Beyond dry. It was raw. "When can I have her diary?"

"I know your type, Mr. Scurto. You pretend to be an ungainly geek but really you are just a smooth-talking player. A gamer. A cheat. Your surface motive is pure but the motor underneath..." He chuckled. "That's a different story."

"I have no secrets," I said. "None."

"Ah." He waved the only waitress over to our table. "You suck at being alone even though you love the idea of being lost in a wilderness. And you claim to be the healthiest eater in the world but you hide burger wrappers under your mattress."

"I don't have a mattress anymore."

"Yes. Because you're homeless. Miss Cuteness," he nodded toward the agave blue-haired waitress. "I'd like my usual and my friend will have a cheeseburger with fries. And bring us the vodka bottle."

"How do you want it cooked?"

He smiled. "Medium."

"Heck no," I said. "Ma'am, make it well done. I'd rather not risk food poisoning."

"Sorry," Miss Cuteness answered me with a crooked grin. "He pays extra to give me orders."

Robbie was silent until the vodka arrived and his glass was poured. He continued to insult me after downing a shot. "You need a mommy figure in your life even if she is also your lover. You are a little boy trapped in a man's body, Scurto. And you want a woman who is capable of doing everything for you while you play outside with the others."

I sniffed the rim of my glass. "There are no others."

"You are a master at playing dumb. Or are you really that stupid?" He poured himself another and raised his eyebrows as he slid out a physical photo of Anna from the inside corner of his shirt. "That you would sacrifice her life to fare better in yours?"

"Where'd you get that picture?" I leaned in as Miss Cuteness set two milkshakes down.

"It's mine," Robbie grinned. He gazed at the eyes in the photo. *My Anna.* "I have my own collection."

"Where? How recent is that picture?"

"Taken eight months before her death. She was so photogenic. Every time."

"Where?"

"You're not the only one who collects hearts, Damon. I'm a master of the game myself."

Miss Cuteness stopped next to Robbie and frowned down at him as she served us the burgers. "Stalk much, hon?"

He winked at her and she clopped back toward the kitchen.

"Scoop's this, buddy. Police records state that I killed her. All the evidence points to me. So why on this Earth would you or anyone else admit to my crime?"

I touched the milkshake straw to my mouth and breathed out. "I carry a murderer's pain."

"So what?"

"I remember so much of her but nothing of how she died or where she was buried."

"You think I have the answers."

"I know you do."

"You think I am innocent."

I did not hesitate. "Yes. I owe you a life sentence."

"You aren't ready to accept fault for any of your misgivings or your cowardice, Mr. Scurto. You have a fragmented memory and perhaps even fabricated bits floating in your brain's sectors."

"A bargain then. I can make a trade."

"And what does Damon Scurto have to offer?"

Nothing. And everything.

4

Castles In Romania

Entry 4.

February 16th, 11:50 am. Bloodthirsty militias and power-hungry dictators. That's what this place is. A curfew in every city with populations over one hundred thousand. The rural land is left to fend in the dark without government aid. Off grid. Foragers. I am trapped in the city, in the sticky heat. Sweat drips down my glasses into my itching eyes.

I see red smoke rising as I pace the terminal windows. Touching the glass burns skin and at night I can see critters of the nocturnal scurrying beyond the walls. It is winter and still there is thick heat from the surrounding factories. Nuclear waste filters through the airport. Miles away from the city there is snow, ice, wind. City limits are set on fire.

Red smoke turning orange and then purple. Fires or flares or symptoms of a militia's fight. Ominous red. Ever ominous. But at least I don't face this alone. Let me introduce you to my airport pals:

Mr. Helmut Richberg. 58 years old. Always in military uniform. Eats paper in the most focused manner and is the sharpest looking of us all. He says I smell the worst. My first and best friend in the airport.

Ms. Lyrna Ickip. 61 years. Sassy silver hair, layered bob cut (which is why I sometimes call her 'bobby-bangs lady'), styles it herself standing in the non-functional body scanner. Most of her day is spent sitting cross-legged on the empty luggage carousel, box of orange crackers in her lap. Crackers are all she eats and anything orange, the woman even wears a tangerine jacket with shoulder pads. Ninety plus degrees all hours and she still cozies up in long sleeves.

Mr. Blintz Garfrinks. 63 years. Cowboy hat over faded auburn hair. Twitching fingers always shuffling something be it cards, toy blocks, or the untouched glasses in the desolate bar areas. Once macho leader material, now falling into the rhythm of mindless ramblings and drumming on the walls with shaky limbs past midnight.

Mr. Chet Whirlgage. 74 years. Rocks back and forth with a broken radio made in the 70s. Sings to a cassette player made in the 80s. Farts like a madman at night. Basically drives us all nuts with his warbling about utopian worlds and what if we had never been nuked. And he wears a pizza box as a hat. (Pizza is a big obsession here, don't know why since we can't find it anymore.)

Mr. Quentin Overdam. 69 years. Obsessed with jigsaw puzzles, calling for a pizza delivery that will never come, and believes we are about to be blown up. Within the first minute of every hour he announces an incoming strike and at the first minute of every hour we stop what we are doing to give him a moment of attention. He is quite gratified by the ordeal even though the missile never comes.

"What are you building this time? A hospital? A control tower?"

"No, it's a tree house."

Mr. Overdam and Mr. Garfrinks were sitting cross-legged on the floor surrounded by plastic toy blocks.

"You know that tree house will fall down too when the bomb hits us."

"The bomb won't hit it."

"It will hit all of us and everything in here."

"No."

"Yes, it will. You said so."

I sat down next to Overdam. "I'd assume you trust your own tower's structure but I could be wrong again."

He looked at me, forehead and brows furrowed. "What are you doing here? You're supposed to be standing watch."

"I don't have to watch. That's Helm's job."

Overdam gave my arm a little push. "Go. Go help him, son. You don't do anything but grumble when you sit down. Go stand. Stand over at the door."

"Hey. I can help make this a sturdier structure here. Give me the blocks."

He continued to hold onto my arm until all of us paused what we were doing and waited for the inevitable.

"Missile! Incoming missile! Get low, they're coming! They're coming, people!"

Overdam ran circles around us before catapulting himself up the busted escalator, leaning over the side and waving the other arm above his head.

"Castles in Romania," we called out in unison. It was our code phrase for him to know we would duck and cover. The whole Quentin Overdam dashing around lasted two minutes then we all carried on as if nothing had been said.

5

Mr. Focus

Entry 5.

February 17th, 4:32 pm. This is what happens when you don't let go of the past. Memories replay over and over on a loop in your head. Specific ones make me nauseous, others make my throat close up, and still others make me scream in anger. What I was accused of. What I carry guilt for. What I did to everyone in my life and the ripples in the river. No one gave me a roadmap, Anna. No one showed me how to be the person you wanted me to be.

I felt safest and happiest behind the wheel of my shiny blue car. Track ready, always kept up to win a prize at a car show or to win me a new hot girlfriend. I nicknamed my ride 'Blue Gem' and I know you treated her just as gentle as I did. You knew I loved my car more than I loved you but not more than I loved myself.

Camille: Damon, I brought a jigsaw puzzle.

Damon: What for?

Camille: I know you love working with your hands while you talk.

Damon: You just assume that after barely knowing me?

Camille: Am I wrong?

Damon: No.

Camille: Do the puzzle. After you take a shower.

Damon: Excuse me?

What is she getting at? Not a shower with her obviously. She is covered neck to ankle in a turtleneck and turd brown curtain of a skirt.

Damon: That's the last thing on my mind today.

Camille: You're disgusting. Sweat is everywhere and you haven't changed clothes.

Damon: So what? We're all gonna die here anyway. The water isn't even on.

Camille: No, the water works here. Use the lounge shower on the third floor.

Fine, therapist. You win.

Camille: Turn on the CD player in the lounge. It's on the counter.

I do what my therapist asks and stand under a torrent of cool, sputtering water. My thoughts float from every ex-lover, you included, and back to my current living situation. I could not have imagined my life would end this way. I could not have imagined I would have to confess things that I barely remember and be forced to cough up emotions I never knew I had.

6

Maryland

Entry 6.

February 18th, 6:19 pm. My family insulted you. Not to your face. They aren't that kind of mean. I guess I get my mean-spirited teasing from them and I suppose it's a very bad thing. I never wanted to acknowledge that I bullied you so much but you told me later how you cried in secret. I brought you home to show you off but no one was impressed. At least not on the first trip.

We should've broken up then, Anna. I wanted to break up with you before that first year was halfway gone. But your sobbing made me rethink. You fell apart in front of me, knowing I had doubts. I'm not good at hiding my disgusted facial expressions.

"Can I ask you something, Scurto?"

"What, Robbie?"

He puffed smoke in my face. "What did she do to you to deserve all that bad company?"

"Nothing."

"Hell no, it must've been something. Was she mean to your mom?"

"No."

"Your grandparents?"

"No. She was really sweet. But also kind of awkward."

"So you insulted your girlfriend when she met your family because she was awkward?"

"I guess I always imagined myself bringing home a tall, exotic, all legs and ass kind of girl. One that loved me, my cars, and you know... one that's like good at cooking and cleaning and stuff."

"So Anna was lazy?"

"No. She did a lot."

"But not enough."

"She didn't wow me, Robbie."

"Wow you? From what I saw of that woman..." He smiled as I frowned. "And believe me, I saw a lot. She was an amazing woman."

"Are you going to repeat that fact every time we meet?"

"I will if you repeat yourself."

"What do you want me to say, Robbie?"

"That your family was wrong about Anna. They treated her like crap and you defended them instead of her."

"Family first."

"Did you love someone else while you were with her?"

"No."

"You're lying."

"Am not."

"Did your therapist touch on that liar instinct of yours yet?"

"I'm not lying."

He rolled his eyes and folded his arms. "Oh, Scurto. You poor dumb—"

"Camille made me listen to sad country music while I took a cold shower. And she ended the session five minutes after I was wrapped in a towel."

"What was that supposed to do?"

"I dunno. She said something about making myself cry to remember why I loved Anna."

"But you never loved her."

"I don't remember that. I was confused. Hence the lack of sobbing in the shower."

"The only therapy that I recommend is what you got in your hand."

I glanced at the bottle I held.

"And," Robbie said, striding over, "it's time you added a new treatment." He cordially took one of his own cigarettes from the pack in his pocket and held it up to my mouth.

"It's been four months since I smoked, Robbie."

"Ya wanna see her grave? Take it."

I nodded once and he lit it for me.

"Now tell me about the trips you took with Anna. Was it as romantic as it was with your first ex?"

"I had high expectations every time I took a girl to meet them. Only one ever met my expectations."

"Not Anna?"

"Not Anna."

"Why did you take her twice then?"

"I didn't want to be alone."

"Yeah, she knew that. One of the last entries in her diary is all about you and your whiny needy self."

"Lemme see it. The diary, Robbie."

He produced the ragged book from behind his back, cradling it above the table. "I will read it to you."

7

On The Track

Entry 7.

February 19th, 2:31 am. I was so proud to have you as my co-pilot, babe. My friends thought you were the most excitable passenger they had ever seen...and then you drove my car. And my heart pounded into my throat. Every time you got behind the wheel, I was nervous for my life. I don't mean to say you were a horrible driver. But you had this thing about being afraid to change lanes at 80 mph and then at a flip of a dime have the urge to show me up with your maniac driving. My second wife, she had skills on the road. I thought that was hot. She was not as sexy as you, but her car skills were fantastic for a woman. I loved that about her.

Lyrna munched her crackers over my shoulder. "Wow, what a jerk. You critique women for everything."

"Go away. I'm writing an entry."

"More like committing suicide with that commentary about the exes."

"Anna's already dead. And Mishele...she's hiding in a bunker that I paid for."

"Where's the first wife?"

"I don't know."

"How do you keep track of one girl and not the others?"

"Certain girls kept my attention longer."

Lyrna started to lean close, touching my computer screen with her bony fingers. "Which ones did that? The kick-ass body, right?"

"No. It was the capable independent spirits." I moved the laptop out of her reach, scooting to a new corner.

"Anna wasn't capable?"

"She had things to figure out before we ever got serious."

"But you never did. You didn't propose to her."

I huffed, took my glasses off, rubbed a hand over my face. "Lyrna, back off. How do you know what I did or didn't say to Anna?"

"I don't like you," she said as she walked away. "I really don't like you."

I rolled my eyes and went back to typing. "Same here, lady. Same here."

8

Puppers

Entry 8.

February 20th, 4:58 pm. I miss having dogs. I miss having a reason to smile. A reason to laugh. Dogs don't judge a person and I was always the best dog dad. I had puppies with Aleya and I dreamed of having a pupper family with you too. Depression got in the way as did Mishele and the dating app discovery. This time Therapist Camille forced me to look at pictures of cute fluffy puppies and it all but made me cry.

Camille: Why are you so emotional, Damon?

Perched on a bar stool dragged from one of the abandoned restaurants, one knee crossed over the other, she looks like a corporate model.

Damon: I miss my dogs.

Camille: When did you have dogs?

Damon: With Aleya. But I walked away from them after we divorced.

Camille: You turned your back on your dogs? Like they watched you leave?

Damon: I had to leave them with her. I couldn't take care of them alone. Didn't have the space or the time as I flew planes.

Camille: You suck at committing to anything. How do you abandon your babies?

Stop making me sad, lady. Sheesh.

Damon: I just did. And they were better than babies. They were supposed to get me through my divorce.

Camille: You have deep issues with bonding. You almost explode with sobs at the sight of puppies yet you walked away from your own dogs years ago. And you claim you miss them. You left them, Damon. You abandoned your family and you went on to ruin other people's lives.

Damn, she's cold.

9

Airplane Food

Entry 9.

February 21st, 12:36 pm. I never ate what you cooked for me. I didn't want you to sweat over a stove if I was uncertain about our future. Robbie calls me stupid for ignoring your gestures of love. He figures I spent more time secretly video-chatting with other women before I dumped you. He is making me feel guilty as we speak...giving me a stink eye as I type this. And then he has this weird fascination with airplane pretzel bags he keeps droning on about. I can't tell if he is being sarcastic or if he really misses airplane food.

"You have a lot to prove, Damon Scurto. One, that you are a killer. And two...did you ever really love her?"

"You don't believe me."

"Your eyes are empty when you say her name."

"No."

"Say it."

"Say what?"

"Say her name."

"Anna."

"Even I have more emotion than that and I wasn't her boyfriend. You lied your entire life to yourself. About what love is and about who really matters to you."

"I tried to fall in love with her. I couldn't."

"Yet supposedly you fell in love with Aleya and Mishele? The two women who dumped you on your ass and ran away? What a crazy outcome for an airhead like you."

"I never told you about them. How do you know their names?"

"Trust me, Scurto, the answer to how I know what I know is not something you want to hear just yet."

"Your secrets aren't helping me get anywhere with finding Anna."

"My game. My rules. I never lie."

"So how did you really get out of prison?"

"I was set free."

"Why?"

"The government needed room for the other bad guys. The ones who slander and backstab the government officials."

"And slander is worse than murder?"

"I didn't make the laws, Flightplan."

I watched him take a cigarette from the inside of his shirt sleeve. He lit it just as Miss Cuteness set down two souvenir glasses of vodka on the table.

"What'd you just call me?"

"Flightplan. You were a pilot, right? You flew planes. Real big ones with hundreds of passengers. Or so I'm told."

"And you assumed that or?"

"Anna's diary. She wrote everything about you in there. The woman's got an eye for detail."

"She wrote about my career? The career that tanked?"

He grinned around the cigarette. "She kept tabs on ya, Flightplan." Then he saw me smirking. "You're wondering what else she says about you. If she was still attracted to you."

I picked up the shot glass and gave him a pointed look.

"Sorry," Robbie said. "Didn't get to that part yet. But that Anna would've made one great spy."

Crap. I totally underestimated you, babe.

"I could have used her street smarts," he went on, "during my law-breaking heyday."

10

Manipulation

Entry 10.

February 22nd, 9:10 pm. No man likes being called a narcissist, control freak, or abuser. When I know love is all I have to give to a woman I don't fancy being called names like that. You still dared to say it in your last letter to me.

"Least she had the guts to say it."

"Please leave me alone, Whirlgage."

"I like a woman who calls me out. Keeps me straight and narrow."

"And you had a woman like that?" I snapped back.

"I did. My wife of fifty years before she died." Whirlgage looked down at his little broken radio. "She knew how to set me right."

"Was she a manipulator?"

"No. She was lovely. You're the manipulator."

"Whirlgage, every man knows they have to be sneaky to get what they want."

"Not me. I was direct," he said.

"You never lied to get your way?"

He shook his head, looking up at me from his seat on the luggage carousel. "Never."

"I'm not the only man to play the game for favors."

"If I may, Scurto, what makes you so conceited?"

"That's a heavy word, Whirlgage."

"It's what you are. You breathe it."

I'm suffocating in this terminal, babe. They are all driving me crazy.

11

Temptress

Entry 11.

February 23rd, 3:32 pm. You're the ghost in the room. What would I have done if I had seen you one last time? They all keep asking me the same two questions. What would I have done? And would it have mattered? Would you be my wife in this world? If only I had told you to stay.

Camille: She forced your hand.

Damon: What do you mean?

Camille: She made you say the words that broke her heart. She made you admit everything.

Damon: I admitted nothing except that I was never in love.

Camille: She knew you had other mistresses behind her back. And I can imagine she viewed herself as just another pretty face as soon as you drove away.

The look on her face is so serious. Too serious. It's giving me a headache.

Damon: I tried to help her feel more confident.

Camille: For who?

Damon: For her. To be happy. To feel sexy like other women.

Camille: And did that pay off?

Damon: I made her stronger.

Camille: By pissing her off and making an enemy?

Damon: I didn't choose to be her enemy. She stayed angry.

Camille: I would've too. You cheated and married that one less than two years after your relationship with Anna.

Damon: I moved on. I fell in love with Mishele for real. I can't help that I didn't love Anna.

Camille: Yet here we are talking about the woman you claim you never truly loved. Why?

Damon: Dreams, therapist. Anna comes to me at night.

12

Inside Jokes

Entry 12.

February 24th, 12:12 pm. Inside jokes. I miss that with you, babe. We were funny together.

"She did have a great sense of humor. There's some funny stuff in here."

"Can I read an entry by myself?"

"Nope."

"Tell me one then. Tell me something funny."

"**Dear diary**," Robbie read, "**I'm so angry at Damon today that I wish I could kick him in the acorns so hard he'd make his own field goal.**"

Facepalm. Really, babe? Really?

"The woman is beautiful, crass, and humorous. I love her."

"And you call me crazy, Robbie. You don't even know her the way I did."

"You don't know what I know. I have a world of secrets about to be given to you for free, Scurto, and if you call me crazy you're gonna lose your chance to hear it."

Dang it. The man is holding all the information I want and the hoops I have to jump through to get it have just been lit on fire. Why am I this desperate, babe? Can't I just wish this guilt away?

"Your conscience is eating you, isn't it?" Robbie said to me. "You're gonna have to live like that until you're dead."

13

Remember Me

Entry 13.

February 25th, 7:32 pm. What help comes from a jaded therapist and a goofy fellowship at the airport? My memories come and go and at times I don't even know if the memories are mine. You know how we make things up just to feel better about the past...I kinda do that. My brain does it without warning like fake or trick psychology. I pretend I never had a ton of girlfriends and that I never was married twice. I pretend that I never met you. And then my airport fellowship has to remind me of how dumb I am. I wonder if you ever tried to forget us.

"Is that her? Dang, she's pretty. You cheated on that thing?"

I grabbed the photo off the floor and put it back in my pocket.

"Thought you didn't have any pictures left of her."

"Robbie gave it to me."

"The serial killer. Of course."

"He's my friend."

"Yeah, really." He hacked a cough onto the back of his hand. "You're a rogue element for sure, bud."

"What does that mean? Are you a rogue element, Richberg?"

"Me? There's a geezer with a pizza box on his head and a grown woman nibbling crackers under a chair. And you think I'm a rogue element?"

I looked around before answering. "Sorry, Rich. I guess eating paper is nothing to be amazed by. Rip me a piece."

"All I got left is a sheet of construction. It's mine."

"C'mon. Lemme chew one."

Richberg frowned as he took the folded-up piece of grey construction paper from his pocket. "All right. A small bit. The rest is mine."

"Fair enough."

We stared at each other as I chewed my first piece of paper and he chuckled at my expression. "Newbie."

14

Landing Gear

Entry 14.

February 26th, 3:51 pm. Flying is the dream I thought I'd never reach. I thought I wasn't capable enough despite all the girls calling me adorable in my uniform when I graduated basic. Supposedly being cute in uniform was going to get me far with the ladies but not so much when it came to moving up in rank.

Camille: Were you a natural pilot?

Damon: I barely made it in.

Camille: How badly did you want it?

She's wearing a pink and grey skirt today matching her blue under-shirt. Kitten heels.

Damon: I couldn't let my mom down.

Camille: But did you do it to make yourself happy?

Damon: I married Aleya to make myself happy.

Camille: What about your career?

Damon: What about it?

Camille: I see. What about the second wife, Mishele?

Damon: She was a surprise. Didn't think I'd find love so quick after dumping Anna.

Camille: Were you happy with her?

Damon: Very much. Ten years of marriage until she ditched.

Camille: And why did she ditch?

Damon: Something about her being tired of doing all the housework and being stuck at home while I got all the free time to be a lazy ass.

Camille: Couldn't be anymore specific?

My therapist is laughing at me or trying not to. I suppose this is part of my punishment for being so mean to you, babe. I'm being mocked at this very moment.

15

Lovies

Entry 15.

February 27th, 1:29 am. There were leftover smells of turkey burger wafting in my apartment. But you did my dishes. You cleaned the shower when I slept...trying to prove you were wifey material. And I said I didn't want you to do any of it. I remember I cried in the kitchen. You had your arms around me as I sobbed, telling me it was okay, that you were here for me, gently stroking my back how a wife would. Your touch was always so soft. You let me cry. I said I didn't want you to leave me...and in the end, Anna, I left you.

16

Wolves

Entry 16.

February 28th, 8:30 pm. My ex mother-in-law gave me my first wolf decoration. It was a lampshade. I kept it in my bedroom on the lamp that my first wife gave me. They liked to indulge my obsession with those animals. You tried to make me smile by buying me presents and sending me packages but honestly I loved the first things I got the most. You tried to copy the wolf theme but it didn't work, did it? I appreciated your efforts, Anna. You never gave up on me.

"Wolves are my favorite animal," I said to no one in particular.

"What's yours, Lyrna?" Richberg asked.

"Poison dart frog."

"Why? Those aren't loveable."

"You can't hug a wolf either."

"Yes, you can." I stood up barefoot on the luggage carousel and looked down at my circle of eccentric friends. "Furry animals get more points than slimy ones."

Lyrna dumped the crumbs from her cracker box onto the floor. "Frogs are the best."

"I'm not about to debate any of you on why wolves are better," I said.

I felt my cheeks redden and a childish shame hit me. "Grown-ups don't talk about their favorite animals."

"You okay, kid?" Whirlgage stared hard at me as I wobbled toward the edge of the carousel.

"You're all annoying," I said with a spray of spit. I wiped the corner of my mouth, pushed up my glasses, and walked quickly to the end of the line of windows.

I have never felt more frustrated in my life, Anna. I don't want to be here. I wish I was back in my house playing video games. Games are much simpler.

17

Orange and Red

Entry 17.

March 1st, 2:22 pm. Camille told me to paint a picture of my past. I painted as you would imagine our life, Anna. I painted you standing outside our log cabin. The trees were red and gold and pumpkin orange with leaves fluttering everywhere. A muddy trail cut through the forest leading to a breathtaking viewpoint on a cliff. You can't see that cliff in my picture but I imagined us standing at the edge, my arms wrapped around your waist, leaning into your cherry blossom scented red hair. You turn into my chest and lift your chin for a kiss as the autumn wind ruffles your form-fitting blouse.

Camille: Keep painting, Damon.

Damon: There's no more canvas.

Camille: Layer it. C'mon. Throw more paint on there.

She circles me and the flimsy easel as I weakly slap my brush over and over against the canvas.

Damon: Everything is turning brown. The mud is running into the trees and the cabin is running into the grass.

Camille: Three points for the tree shapes, but your Anna looks horrible.

I turn around and flick red paint toward her.

Damon: No one is good at painting bodies.

Camille: Serves you right. Anna looks just as bad in the painting as you probably made her feel. The world around her is beautiful but she is too beat up to notice it.

Damon: That's very rude, therapist.

Sorry I suck at painting your arms and legs, Anna. At least I got your wild red hair right.

18

Homewrecker

Entry 18.

March 2nd, 12:24 pm. Two ex-wives. And Robbie wanted me to give him their numbers. A favor for his helping me get to you. I'm sort of dumb. Not only is my memory patchy but so is my rate of quick wit. You would say I never had good humor.

"Either of them single?"

"Last I heard Aleya didn't remarry."

"I'll take her number in place of cash." He picked a small bronze cross from his front shirt pocket and slid it across the table. "To help you find the grave."

"You already know where she is buried."

"Do I? See, Flightplan, I may need more convincing to get you access to a plane. I think after all the torture you put poor Anna through, you need to be tortured back."

"I am being tortured. You sitting here looking at her pictures and reading her diary out loud is killing me."

Robbie grinned. "See? Karma. And I thought you weren't the jealous type."

"Fine. Here's Aleya's number. Just don't call her in front of me."

He took the piece of paper, holding it awkwardly between his middle and ring finger. "If that isn't a challenge, I don't know what is."

19

Our Country Song

Entry 19.

March 3rd, 1:18 am. When I was a kid I listened to the country oldies. Through my late teen years, it changed as I tried to become a ladies' man in the society that I assumed thrived on fast shiny cars and rap music. You brought country music back to me, Anna. I thank you for that. Thank you for teaching me to sing again no matter how wrong the lyrics were. You could sing well. You were my little redhead cowgirl tigress.

20

Numbers

Entry 20.

March 4th, 4:08 pm. I always liked the women with long straight hair. Both of my ex-wives had straight hair. You were the only one I ever dated who had the bouncy curls...long curls, but very wild. I guess I have a problem with looking for perfection? I don't know. Camille thinks I'm like super picky with hair type and eye color. Today she did this picture exercise with me rating every single photo that she held up to the light of the airport windows. We sat cross-legged three feet apart from each other on the carpet, bowls of half-eaten ramen at our sides.

Camille: This one?

Damon: She's a ten.

Camille: And this one?

Damon: Four.

Camille: How is she that much lower than the last? Same hair type, same lips, same eye color.

Damon: Different jaw structure, the last one had dimples in her smile, and this one doesn't apply eyeliner the right way.

Camille: Heaven help you.

Damon: What? I'm being honest.

Camille: That's not honesty. It's pure criticism.

Damon: I'm just trying to help them look better.

Camille: To what standards?

Damon: The world.

Camille: World, my ass. It's all about looking hot for you.

Damon: I didn't marry hot women.

Camille: Aleya and Mishele weren't hot?

Damon: I take it back. Aleya was a ten.

Camille: And Anna? Where was she on the scale?

Damon: Six.

21

Smokin' Boots

Entry 21.

March 5th, 1:13 pm. Hot women have a hold on me. This I know to be true. Ever since Robbie showed me the photo of his late lover Marga I had her face in my head overriding yours. He was reluctant to give me the pictures found in the pages of your diary and I know it is because of how he sees me as a cheating bastard, a pathetic womanizer. But I finally got him to give me the pictures. The pictures of you in your happy state before I broke your heart.

"You know what Anna reminds me of? An Elf. A really pretty and well-built Elf princess. You get me? Like one of those fantasy movie warriors with the long red hair and perfect little curves in the right places. Except she rocks the long curly hair instead of pin straight hair that you slobber over so much. I can totally picture her in spiked heel boots. So smokin' hot."

I took a drag and nodded at Robbie. He was laying on the diner floor with his feet propped up against the counter between two tattered bar stools. *He had a smug smile on his face as he fantasized about you, Anna. So annoying.* "I get ya, Rob."

"You're lucky I gave you those pictures. I've had them for so long. Makes me smile."

"Did you really get the diary from her grave?"

"I never dug anything up. Someone left it sitting on the dirt so I took it right after the service."

"Who would leave her diary on top of a burial mound? Why would someone abandon such a private book?"

"Death changes everything, Flightplan. You know that. Rational behavior dissipates in the aftermath of human grief."

I picked at the soggy fish sandwich on my plate, staring into the wisps of cigarette smoke. "I can't believe you were at Anna's funeral."

"It's easy to pretend you are at a cemetery for someone else. I spent a good while reading the tombstones when I was there that day. A few of them were murder victims."

My stomach dropped. "How did you know that?"

Robbie smiled far too big before he answered me. "Friends of mine were trained to kill too. They always bragged to me about their hunt."

I accidentally sucked in a cloud of smoke and coughed hard.

"The cops thought I was violent," Robbie said, "but I had pals who were far worse."

"Who killed more often?"

"I was usually the bait for the victims. Being handsome helps when shadowing beautiful women."

"That's terrible," I said.

"Join the club, Flightplan."

22

Cornholin'

Entry 22.

March 6th, 9:19 pm. We were gonna be partners in a game that day. I asked if you would be on my team. You backed away from me so fast, eyes downcast. You seemed to know I had already moved on and in fact I had but I never ever wanted to speak the truth. I just wanted to hold onto our friendship as I made love with a new woman. I wanted to use you and her together.

Here's the thing, Anna. I love games. I love having fun and laughing and tickling and play wrestling with my women. We would've been great country lovers if I had kept you next to me. We could've played cornhole with my family and at our wedding reception.

"Lyrna, if you flick one more cracker into this cup so help me—"

"All right, all right. This game is stupid anyway."

"It's not stupid. It's a classic."

I chimed in as I ate my ramen several feet from their layout. "You made it up this morning."

"Your slurping is really wrecking my focus, Scurts."

"I can see your butt crack from here, Richberg."

"Bite me!" Lyrna shouted and trotted off.

Ah, the soundscape of the airport. By the way, I officially named the journal on my computer. I'm titling it Scurts Flightplan in honor of Helmut Richberg, who calls me Scurts, and Robbie Decker, who calls me Flightplan. I figure all this typing needs a title – otherwise it's just rambling without a purpose.

23

Dirt Of The Dead

Entry 23.

March 7th, 2:20 am. Don't tread on the dirt of the dead. It will get you possessed or at the least force you to scrub yourself down with holy water. So much I don't remember, and yet the most vivid memories are as loud as the gunfire that pops outside when the officers hunt down stragglers breaking curfew. Seeing your grave will be a privilege, babe, and I know you didn't take death lightly. I know you became an angel and I hope you are lighting up the entire cemetery with your new heavenly glow. You tried to save me from the darkness of the bleak and fiery underworld and yet I persisted in seeking out the shadows instead of Heaven.

24

War Movie

Entry 24.

March 8th, 12:39 pm. Even the most predictable person can do something completely unexpected when given enough time.

"She didn't have a violent bone in her body."

"That's a lie, Flightplan. You thought she was crazy."

"She was emotional at best. Hot-headed at worst."

"You thought she was crazy," he said flatly.

"Absolutely bonkers," I said.

Robbie leaned forward and crunched a chip in my face. "They always are."

"Is it just me or do you like crazy women too?"

"It's just you. My Marga was the opposite of a tempest. She was a cloudless starry night glazed in moonbeams."

"You're lying."

"I never lie. She was a doll. When she got angry it was all a silent war front. She was loud in every other mood though."

"So she never picked a fight?"

"The only fight she picked with me was a tickle fight."

I smiled down at the coffee cup. "Cute."

Robbie snapped his gum while he cut up the sausages on his plate. "What would you have done if she had attacked you?"

"Anna, attack me? Nothing."

"Would you have fought back?"

"No. I don't know."

"What if she had gone after your exes?"

"No." I shook my head, facing the window. "No, she wasn't that crazy."

"How do you know that, Flightplan?" His next words came out in a sudden crescendo then dropped to a sly whisper. "You didn't read her diary."

What is in that thing, Anna? What did you really say about me?

"She was capable of retribution. But she loved you too much to actually pull off a violent retaliation."

Tell me.

"Listen up, bud," Robbie said loudly. He started to read an entry.

Anna's Diary: You don't know this but I sat outside your apartment tonight, Damon. I sat in the driver's seat, all other seats empty as I stared straight ahead at the rain shuffling against my windshield. I remember which apartment is yours and I know you are with her. I think you would've liked my retro, edgy outfit...four silver hoop earrings, short as heck denim skirt over black fishnet tights, spiked black thigh high boots, and a trendy black leather jacket zipped halfway over my body-hugging black and red shirt.

My makeup is as dark as you could imagine it and I put on fake nails just for tonight...I have a walking stick on my lap. I grip it tightly as I glance in the rearview mirror. Wondering. Grieving. Filled with everything but happiness. All I want is revenge. All I want is payback. One last war cry.....I can't do this....

25

Gamer

Entry 25.

March 9th, 10:11 pm. Fine. I admit it. I was addicted to gaming. I can't say it was an escape, baby, but it was a release for my anger. You never saw me lose my temper the way Aleya and Mishele saw it. I tried to protect you from my bad moods by acting out my rage on screen. Shooting aliens and zombies and evil cowboys helped for a few hours a day until depression increased my anxiety and stress and I found myself playing games until sunrise.

"Your turn to make a card tower, Scurto."

"Can you think of anything less boring in here? How about sliding down the escalator railing?"

"Say it's a race and I'm in."

That's what we did out of pure boredom. Using what little healthy brains we had left to create childish games to play in the whole of the airport. We had easy access to at least two of the floors in the terminal and when we felt adventurous enough some of us would wander either lower or higher through mazes of twisted metal on the very end of the structure to glimpse the rare sighting of government-sanctioned water trucks lining up on the crumbled highway.

26

Capable

Entry 26.

March 10th, 1:42 am. Life will never be fair. Also, being happy all the time is a darn pipe dream. I was depressed enough times in my existence to be empty of empathy when you came along. You tried to make me happy and you tried to prove you were worthy of being my next wife. I'm sorry I hurt you, Anna. But I'm not sorry for showing you what I wanted. A capable woman is a strong, emotionless, caretaker of a man...kind of like my mama was.

27

Wolf Necklace

Entry 27.

March 11th, 11:04 am. I gave it to you because I wanted to show you my love.

"Actually, Flightplan, I hate to burst your bubble but after she thought the gesture was sweet and romantic she began thinking you had a dark motive. She wrote in her diary that she thought the wolf necklace was a sign of you trying to own her body."

"I saw her wear it every day we were together."

"And when you betrayed her, she destroyed it. Ah," Robbie said from behind the diary. "Listen to this entry: **You gave me your hoodie**."

"No, she kept it," I muttered as I dug into my pancakes.

"Then she wrote that you took her hat."

"I bought it for her."

Anna's Diary: I felt like you owned me when you put that wolf pendant around my neck. It made me feel like I was the only woman in your world. It made me feel special. But there was a darkness that came with the necklace...a weight I couldn't shake each morning as I rolled over in bed to put it on. It's like you had a hold on me and you knew it. You manipulative jerk.

You made me crave you even when you chased other girls. You fooled all of us. You made us all feel like your queens when in fact you broke every heart. I wore that dang necklace from the day you sweetly put it around my neck and kissed me until a month after it was over. Your spell is broken, Damon Scurto. I'm rid of your darkness.

28

Dancing In Apartment

Entry 28.

March 12th, 8:04 pm. Take all the synthesizers in the world and put them together and we get your favorite dance jam, huh, babe? You were my retro girl. Dance like the 80s, dress like the 90s. I'll never forget watching The Breakfast Club with you. You were so cute dancing to all the music in the living room while I sat on the couch with my laptop and leftover fast food curly fries. I watched you dance when you didn't know I was looking. I watched you all the time.

"Do you think he knows we're watching?"

"Give him another two minutes."

"This popcorn is stale."

"Every food scrap in the terminal is stale."

I stopped mid-spin with one arm in the air. All five of them were watching. Lyrna and Richberg had bags of popcorn.

"Nice dance moves, Scurts. Anna teach you that?"

"It's just the…" I gestured to the cassette player on the floor. "The music reminds me of her."

"80s rock. Good stuff, son," Whirlgage said.

I didn't want to talk anymore that night, but I also didn't want them all to watch me embarrass myself with my lousy dancing. I silently picked up the cassette player and for the first time during my life in the airport, I left my laptop on the floor as I turned my back to my eccentric pals. I found a new secret spot to air-guitar alone.

29

Thank You For Loving Me

Entry 29.

March 13th, 3:39 pm. When I became distant you saw right through me. You saw I was a bad guy. The transparency in you devastated my ego to the last bit and I could never ever measure up to what you imagined me to be. The man you saw in me didn't exist and you loved me still. How do you go on after so many lies? How do you learn to love again, Anna? Did you ever try?

Camille: I never got married. The commitment scared me too much.

Damon: So you understand the risks.

Camille: Not enough to cheat.

Damon: How many men did you say I love you to?

Camille: One.

Damon: Then you know it's a rare spark.

Camille: How did you not fall in love with the woman who did everything for you?

Damon: Her doing things was not meant to make me fall in love. Nothing makes a man fall for a woman. It just happens. You're a therapist. You would know that.

Camille: You knowingly tortured her heart, Damon. You're a tease.

Damon: Thank you, therapist. I'm living with this guilt now.

30

Freeway Rain

Entry 30.

March 14th, 6:20 pm. I remember when we shared a ride to the airport and the way you held my hand...yours were cold. The driver enjoyed conversing with us, not realizing how googly-eyed we were for each other in his back seat. I remember being so happy with you next to me, happy bringing you to meet my family. And then it all changed when we got there.

"So why didn't they like her? She sounds like the perfect woman."

"I know, Robbie. I'm not stupid."

He laughed into his beer. "I think you kinda are, pal. She was wifey material period."

"We've been over this."

"And your memory is going to fade completely one day."

"So is yours. You get high so much it's gonna wipe your memory too."

"I can't believe they didn't like her. I still don't believe that. She was an incredible woman."

I responded with my eyes closed. "Can you stop saying she was an incredible woman?"

"No. You don't say it so someone has to. That someone here is me. Get it? Got it."

"Would you change the subject? How about the new street regula-
tion?"

"You mean the one about not looking a government official in the eye
or you'll be peppered with lead? Yeah."

"No. The one where we have to carry our own hand-crank nuclear
sirens."

"Sorry, Scurto. I'd much rather talk about your lovely ex-girlfriend
who, by the way, I know way too much about."

31

Chocolate Cherries

Entry 31.

March 15th, 11:21 pm. Traditions die hard, Anna. Remember those years you enjoyed the chocolates and cheeses my grandparents sent me for New Year's? One of my favorite memories of us...and it's been over for decades. Right now we're all laying down in the pitch black terminal playing another one of Helmut Richberg's dumb inspirational word games.

"Real soldiers do not sit on their asses waiting for love to be dished out to them in the form of turkey burgers and chocolate cherries."

"Words to live by, Richberg," Lyrna said around a mouthful of crackers. She raised her hand. "I have one."

"Go, girl."

"Wait," I said. "I swear you stole that from my laptop. No one else here likes chocolate cherries."

"Did your grandma really make them by hand?" Lyrna asked me.

"No, she did not. They were store bought. I got them in the mail every year."

"What's chocolate and cherry taste like?"

"Stop asking questions, lady," I said to Lyrna. "Your voice is really annoying."

"So is yours."

"Who keeps farting? I can't tell if that's my own bum quaking or someone else radiating through the floor."

"Whirlgage, that's you."

This night can't be over fast enough, Anna. What am I doing here laying on a dirty airport carpet in nothing but sticky jeans, sweating from head to toe? I used to have a life, right? I used to be cool. I had a family who wrote me cards and sent me care packages across the country. What happened, babe? It's punishment, isn't it? I think you put a curse on me.

32

Sirens and Gobbling Turkeys

Entry 32.

March 16th, 2:54 am. Outside my apartment at night I could always hear those ambulance sirens flying by toward the highway. And then there were the turkeys. I swear every time it was either midnight or four in the morning, they made their obnoxious noise and swarmed the entire apartment complex like a feathered army alerting the sleeping victims to danger. I miss those stupid turkeys right now. All I can hear is paper spitting, cracker crunching, dice rolling, and mumbling of all types in the terminal. Every sound echoes in a way that seems otherworldly. Just please, God, send a blaring ambulance straight through the windows and let there be a yammering male turkey flapping around on top of it.

33

Tattoo

Entry 33.

March 17th, 12:09 pm. I'm a big baby with needles. Anything sharp actually. Apparently Robbie loves pain...he is covered with tattoos. He said you had two full sleeves of ink when you were put in the ground.

"What were they of?"

"What of?"

"Her tattoos. You said you saw her tattoos."

"I only saw one in person. It was a black and grey war tank on her left forearm."

"What kind of tank?"

"Flightplan, how long were you with her?"

"Two years."

"And you never learned that she loved military aircraft and vehicles?"

"We watched a lot of war movies and documentaries, but I was the one who bought magazines on plastic model war machines. She always looked the other way in the bookstore."

"Probably because you were ignoring her and casting a flirty gaze at some sexy nerd at the coffee corner."

"No." I was indignant. "I loved when we went to look at books

"

together. It was our thing."

"So you never noticed that she loved war tanks? And that was without you talking her into liking them, by the way."

"What kind of tank, Robbie?"

He hesitated, looking behind me at the clock above the cook's station, counting every second. "M18," he finally said.

"Hellcat." I grinned, picturing what that ink would have looked like. "Dang, that's cool."

Robbie hunched over his milkshake sipping on three neon-colored straws. "Apparently she only got the courage to get the tats after you broke her heart. Far as I'm concerned, it was the best decision she made for herself." He closed his eyes as he went on, a smile spreading from one cheek to the other. "She really rocked ink."

"Stop fantasizing about my ex."

"You didn't even try to keep her from walking away!"

"She left because I told her I was done."

"Yeah, because you already replaced her with Mishele."

"I did not."

"I beg to differ."

34

Heart In A Jar

Entry 34.

March 18th, 1:15 pm. Every time you left my apartment doorway, it was the same exchange of 'I love you' and 'I'll miss you'. But when I shut the door and you were well on your way home driving that night highway two-hour trip...I opened a video chat with a new woman. If you knew anything, it was from your own suspicions, babe. I never left evidence of my unfaithfulness.

"You say you never cheated on a woman, fine. But I don't believe you, Flightplan. Not for a second."

"So?"

"Any man who got the smooth-talking down like you do can melt and break a heart. You are one of those stealthy jerks who destroys a woman just as she gives her body and love to you...then you decide you can't fall in love, aren't in love, tell her after teasing her with a ring and pretend you are the victim while she cries her eyes out on the drive home."

"I don't do that. I never did."

"The lies coming out of you are slick as oil. Ignorant too."

"You don't know me, Robbie. You haven't been in my head."

"It's the evidence you don't leave that leads a woman to suspect cheating. Normally messy room becomes clean. Normally messy clothes pile? Folded and hung up. Normally lounging on the couch with your laptop? Walking around smelling like cologne and body wash, reorganizing furniture and switching out wall art. That's how she reads cheating."

"Please stop. I get it." I lit a cigarette.

"The books she gave you for Christmas? No longer on your coffee table. Usually depressed and sulking in bed? Then up and smiling and giddy when you weren't around her for weeks. Yeah, she knows you replaced her then. Secrets make you smile like an idiot."

"I don't have as many secrets as you think."

"You smile every time you lie, Flightplan. The glee on your face gives it all away. It's an awful reason to smile."

"You must have smiled each time you committed a crime."

"I was dead serious in my actions," Robbie said. "It was never a game."

35

Daddy Issues

Entry 35.

March 19th, 2:43 am. There's so much you didn't know about me, babe. So much I didn't tell you. I was afraid you'd leave me. No man wants to admit he has issues with the other men in his family. A lack of morality, lack of trust, and lack of love created the shadowed person that is me. I saw things at eight years old that no little kid should see and it wasn't the rated R stuff that scarred me, it was the countless women flowing in and out of my childhood home that shaped me into who I am.

I was taught to view women as pleasure-givers, numbers, and as angelic beings who are here to make us happy all the time. It is a flawed logic according to all the therapists I had. It turned me into an aloof and falsely loving monster. But I was just copying what the men in my life had done.

36

Hit Me

Entry 36.

March 20th, 1:43 pm. Revenge is best served warm...so says my associate Robbie Decker. Otherwise you wait too long and they forget why you were angry in the first place. Anger dissolves into insanity.

"She thought glasses were sexy, Flightplan. You always trash talked yourself. She said she was sad when you wore contacts instead of glasses."

"My choice, my problem."

"But why not please her when she spent three hours doing her hair and makeup for you?"

"I didn't tell her to do that."

"You did. It's called subtle manipulation. You were the king of it."

"I wanted to teach her to look as good as the other women her age."

"Why was she not good enough on her own?"

"She needed to learn things. I felt like I was put in her life to teach her."

"According to her words you were a complete jerk half the time. The fact that she stayed so long is beyond me."

"Her emotions went deeper than mine. She was sensitive."

"Sensitive?" Robbie sounded extra surprised. "And you aren't sensitive? You don't even like women crying in front of you but you cried in front of them all the time. You were a big baby."

"How did you know that I cried?"

"Anna wrote an entry about that. She said you covered her silk shirt with snot and tears. That's gross, Flightplan. Whatever happened to being a real man?"

"Crying shows a soft side, Robbie. Women like men who cry. They think it's cute and when I do get emotional it helps them to know how to fix me."

"You admit you cry to get your way." Robbie grinned and laughed into his beer, almost falling over. "That's so sad."

37

Crazy Eyes

Entry 37.

March 21st, 9:48 pm. You had this way of staring into my eyes. It gave me chills in the way gripping a live wire would. The shock of your gaze thrilled and exhausted, calmed and terrified. If I miss one thing the most, baby, it's your eyes. Your chocolate pudding eyes.

"Chocolate pudding? Really? There are better ways to describe a woman's brown eyes."

Overdam sat behind me, squinting at what I had just typed. "I thought you said she had real crazy eyes."

"I said—"

"I had a different name for my girl's crazy eyes."

I nodded and flicked a puzzle piece in his direction. "F," I stated.

"Shhh. Not that word. No, no, no I never said that."

"Then what did you call your girl's crazy eyes?"

His dentures started to slide forward as he grinned. "I called it the Brace For Impact stare. Those were my doll's crazy eyes."

"That sounds stupid. No disrespect."

"Son, all you do is disrespect. Weren't you taught honor by your parents?"

"Honor doesn't exist in this life, Overdam. You need to fix your teeth."

"Gonna lie down and sleep in an hour. I don't need to keep my teeth in."

"Ugh." I waved him off as I stood up and clutched my laptop under my arm. "I'm gonna go upstairs."

Spittle flew everywhere as old man Overdam called after me and his dentures dropped out mid-sentence. "Watch out for spiders in the escalator. They come out from between the steps."

38

Car Talk

Entry 38.

March 22nd, 12:31 am. Even though you weren't a huge car enthusiast I remember how much you loved listening to me gab about my shimmery metal babies. Yes, I married a car freak after I dumped you and then she turned out to be a cheater and dumped me but I really miss seeing you light up in the garage looking all cute in your red flannel and country girl jeans. You kept me company during all my track days and whenever we went to get my cars washed you happily came along. I know some of my friends thought you were adorable but I never told you. I guess I just wanted you for myself.

39

Proper Place

Entry 39.

March 23rd, 1:28pm. I'll go to hell if I don't change my ways. You always hated when I said that out loud. I don't know if I ever truly believed my own words. I don't know if I ever believed in God. I've always been scared of dying alone...but afraid of going to hell? I doubt there is a proper place for me after all I've done.

"I carry Psalms with me," Robbie said. "Only part of the Bible I've ever read and understood. Real poetry."

"You don't seem the type to like poetry. Possibly one who sprays graffiti on the walls outside though."

"Not the only one to do that, bud."

"We all have things we aren't proud of," I said.

"Sure. Like my two dozen robberies, four assaults, and seven murders. But I confessed and I paid my debt. I don't have nightmares over it."

"I deserve peace too."

I'm tired, Anna. I want to sleep.

"Peace comes in the afterlife, Flightplan. I created agony in the lives of innocent people for years before I came to justice. But earthly justice is not the same. Gonna be different up there." He pointed to the ceiling.

"Robbie," I said, "I doubt that's where you're going."

"You don't believe in miraculous conversions?"

"No. I don't believe in miracles."

40

Delayed Flight The Overnight

Entry 40.

March 24th, 11:13 pm. I listen for planes at night, pressing my hands against the glass as I watch military crafts take-off. Sometimes seeing a plane lift into the sky churns my emotions and the memory of our night stuck in the airport comes to mind. It was supposed to be earlier that day, but we had landed late and missed the last flight home...booking for the early morning left us roaming the terminal from dinner time til sunrise. You didn't sleep a wink. I remember laying down with my backpack as a pillow and you refused to lay down next to me. You crazy girl, Anna. You paced that airport all night. I never forgot that.

41

Accountable

Entry 41.

March 25th, 4:25 pm. You never take responsibility she tells me. You never want to admit your faults. She is right, of course. But I don't want to answer to a higher power either. Therein lies the bigger problem. Camille reminds me of how much I did to hurt you and in the end it turns out I should have given everything over to God up there in the sky. I could have saved everyone from pain if only I had prayed fervently and actually believed in something bigger than me. I never ever wanted to let someone else rule over my life. I never wanted someone to tell me what to do. I make my own choices. I always have.

Camille: You never ask for directions in life.

Damon: I never want directions.

Camille: You claim to believe in a higher power but have you ever trusted in it?

Damon: Miracles aren't real.

Camille: Wasn't Aleya a miracle? Mishele? Your mom and grandparents? Didn't a higher power provide them for you?

Damon: That's not a miracle.

Camille: They stood by you through a thousand shitstorms. Why couldn't you accept advice from Anna? What made her unworthy in the capacity to hold you accountable? Every person needs someone to keep them in check. Anna sounded loving, trusting, available to you at all hours if you needed her.

Damon: She was.

Camille: Isn't that the definition of true loyalty and love?

42

Aleya and Mishele

Entry 42.

March 26th, 6:12 pm. I never intend to break a woman's heart. But, yes, I do hurt people. We all do it, Anna. Even you. You accused me of something I never had the balls to do. I never cheated on my women. I was a good man. I will admit to engaging in video chats with other women behind your back, but I never considered it cheating. I still call it playful conversation. My intention was never to create resentment in you.

"I'm sorry, Flightplan, did you really just type that?"

"Yeah. It's my journal."

"You said you never cheated. You're still telling yourself that? You're convinced that emotional cheating is not cheating and that kissing another woman before you dump the current one is not cheating?"

"Yes."

"You thought you could stay friends with Anna even though you smashed her heart."

"Yes. I stay friends with all my exes. I did."

"You think all women are understanding of a wandering guy's soul? That's just idiotic."

"The ones who do understand have lower standards."

"Ah, so you do like the bad girls."

"I like the girls who make me feel wanted."

"Flightplan, you had everything with the woman you said was not girly enough and yet you picked a woman who was more of a man than you are."

"I'm sorry, what?" I said.

Robbie jumped up on the table and did an impromptu tap dance before pointing at me. "Fail. You lost the princess warrior to gain the bossy mommy."

"Mishele wasn't bossy." I smiled to myself. "Only a little."

"She wore the pants, didn't she? Anna was actually willing to follow you, but you wanted a woman to walk you around like a puppy."

"I don't like being in charge."

"And how has that worked out for you, Flightplan? I'd say it's been a disaster."

I raised my voice as Robbie cackled and sputtered vodka all over the table. "It's not funny."

"Your love life is the most hysterically ridiculous story I've ever heard."

43

About Nothing

Entry 43.

March 27th, 1:03 am. Sometimes I wake up and sit in the pitch dark of the terminal listening to Lyrna's munching, Richberg chewing and spitting wads of paper, and the soft clatter of puzzle pieces being dropped from the second floor as Overdam tried to make one bounce. When we were at our most bored, we would make up games, like practicing different goofy styles of walking on top of the luggage carousel.

"Drunk sailor. Do the drunk sailor!" Lyrna would always call out to Richberg.

"I got the wedding wobble down. Watch me."

"Whirlgage, stick with the farting toucan. That's your best move."

I raised my hand as I stared at my laptop screen. "Count me in. I'll do the bouncing cow."

Yeah, it gets really weird here at night. Like embarrassingly weird. Enough said.

44

Where She Is

Entry 44.

March 28th, 4:37 pm. I always wondered how I'd fare in a jail cell. I think I'd be one of those inmates who gets used to feeling trapped but at the end of the day sketch out a little escape plan on whatever surface I could find.

Today I sit with my back to the windows, knees pulled up to my chest, repetitively rolling dice on the carpet. Camille stares at me as she sits in her makeshift executive chair, staring as she scribbles and erases on her legal pad.

Camille: Damon, take a walk with me.

Damon: Where we walking?

Camille: Runway.

Damon: It's gross and hot out there.

Camille: Walk with me. I need you to see a billboard.

Damon: I thought all of those were burned down.

Camille: Come.

I follow her outside into the sticky air. Sweat drips down into my eyes so I take off my glasses and hold them. My bare feet burn on the ground, stink of the calloused sweat sizzling off my soles.

Damon: What are we looking at?

She points far to the left beyond the crisscross highways and decades old debris.

Camille: That billboard has a familiar face on it, doesn't it?

Damon: Missing woman.

The face on the sign is yours, Anna. After all this time, I see your fiery red hair and sweet brown eyes on a giant rectangle in the middle of carnage.

Camille: They never took it down. Even after Robbie Decker was convicted and her funeral occurred. Her face stayed.

Damon: What do you want me to think?

Camille: The void in your heart is right there. She is just a memory. A picture. You can't hold her anymore. You gave up that pleasure the minute you told her to leave.

Damon: I never told her to go anywhere.

Your eyes make me emotional, Anna. What happened all those years? Where did you go? Where did you live?

Camille: You had moved on. She walked away because there was no love in you, and at the very end, she acknowledged that. And so did you.

45

Running, Running, Running

Entry 45.

March 29th, 12:41 pm. We tried. We tried to keep our heads above water. Our hearts above relationship hell. I often think of the drive we made in the rental car from the Pittsburgh airport to the western part of Maryland. I watched you take so many pictures through the car windows...you took them of everything, even boring highway bridges. The world that I had come from was foreign to you. The adventure in your eyes was adorable. Yet I remember thinking I couldn't keep it up. I couldn't keep running away from the truth.

"She said she started running after the break-up. Like two months after you dumped her. I ended up crossing paths with her during my own walkabout in the neighborhood and asked her about her day, what she was up to and she ranted."

"Why would she talk to you? You were a stranger."

Robbie shrugged. "She needed to vent."

"Why would Anna vent to a strange man?"

"I wasn't a stranger. We had a history."

"You knew her." I repeated the words in my head.

"Yeah," he said. "I have a connection to Anna."

"When did you meet her the first time?"

"That's another day's revelation, Flightplan."

"Where? Tell me."

"I went to college with her. She was barely an acquaintance."

I touched the inside of my right wrist, feeling my pulse shoot up.

"What did you do with her, Robbie?"

"I tried to be her friend."

46

Barefoot Sunday

Entry 46.

March 30th, 2:14 am. You showed me the beauty of church people, Anna. You showed me the hope of a family and of a future with you. Maybe a little girl running barefoot across the fake grass of a church pavilion. I'd build us a house and decorate the backyard for Bible study barbecue nights. All our friends would hang out late into the night laughing and we'd trade flirty smiles whenever we were several feet apart stuck in the middle of another conversation.

47

Sins Of A Cheater

Entry 47.

March 31st, 4: 21 pm. Used and abused. That's what therapist Camille calls you. Said you were my temporary angel until I broke your wings. She said I held you in the wrong light. I called you crazy when you were just being emotional and you were like any normal woman who would react to being dishonored. I still prefer a cool-headed woman like Mishele was. She never threw a tantrum at me.

Camille: You don't punch the angel that was sent to help you, dear.

Damon: Indeed.

Camille: You compare every woman with flings of the past. Then you tell them to wear the same clothes that your exes did.

My involuntary smirk is a reflex. Truth.

Camille: Sometimes it takes the end of the world for the most confident person in the world to realize he is not in control.

Damon: I wish I had more control of anything in my life.

Camille: You could've chosen not to cheat on Anna. God knows how many more times you cheated on other women.

I glower. I take off my glasses and set them on the floor next to where I sit cross-legged with my laptop.

Damon: I am not a cheater.

Camille: All sins are forgiven but never forgotten.

Damon: Heaven doesn't hold grudges.

Camille: Have you committed anything worse outside of cheating and lying? Have you stolen? Murdered?

Damon: I did steal once. It was right after the nuclear attack amidst the carnage in the streets. This one gas station had every window blown out of it, there was glass everywhere. I followed a group of kids in there and without hesitation I twisted the cap off a soda bottle from the busted fridge and drank it in front of the dazed cashier.

I shrug as I feel my cheeks grow warm.

Damon: I guess it wasn't really a crime.

Camille: Regardless of the circumstance, Damon, you wouldn't be behind bars anyway. Your friend Robbie Decker was set free under the new law as was every other conventional criminal. We might as all be criminals for our sins.

Damon: What are your sins?

She sips her wine extra slow.

Camille: I've stolen every piece of clothing I wear. Eighteen hours after the nuclear attack I ran shoe-less, bare-faced, in pajamas, out of my condo straight down two miles to the closest shopping center. I busted a few windows and within a few minutes of pulling off racks I had my arms full of any and every clothing item I could carry. I spent thirteen minutes on my hands and knees in a makeup department sifting through products, including one small bottle of a cherry blossom perfume.

She takes the little perfume bottle from her jacket pocket and holds it up. She smiles at me.

Camille: I never wear this. It just reminds me I'm a pretty woman. That I came from class.

Damon: So you aren't as moral as you appear, therapist.

Camille: When is morality counted at the end of the world, Damon?

I can't help thinking, Anna, that even in the midst of chaos and violence you would be the one to offer all of your food to a scared person covered in rubble and blood.

Camille: We are all scared.

She's reading my mind, babe. She knows too much of how I think.

48

Standing Down

Entry 48.

April 1st, 12:53 pm. Robbie believes in fighting anyone to get what he wants. He believes in a world war. He says peace is an illusion, that we can never just get along. He says I'm insane to believe in doing nothing. But I would rather live and die a quiet life of pleasure. You remember how we argued, Anna? I saw how hot-blooded you were at your core. You always yelled and cried about some cause close to your heart while I thought it was just a waste of energy. Maybe that's why we failed. Maybe that's why you died...if only you controlled your passion. Your temper couldn't be stilled. Robbie Decker thinks you were the smart one. He says I am nothing but wishy-washy, aloof. Bullshit.

"I care more of her worth than you ever did. Anna should've been allowed to scream at you. She should have hit you."

"And what would I have done?"

"You would've let her win. The woman deserves revenge."

I would never fight back, Anna. I am not confrontational. I will always stand down.

49

Steadfast

Entry 49.

April 2nd, 4:01 am. Can you imagine me, Damon Scurto, running headfirst into a wall of rifle fire? I doubt I would last three minutes on the front line. I wasn't built for war or protecting a woman. I'm terrified of having to defend what's mine. I want the woman I love to defend me first. You, Anna, were a spitfire. A steadfast warrior among airhead chicks. Your mental strength outweighed mine and your dreams intimidated me. I could never keep up with a woman so strong. You were someone willing to fight for what you wanted when I was one to back down. I backed down every time.

50

What Is Written

Entry 50.

April 3rd, 4:33 pm. Camille made me try a new exercise today. She told me to close my eyes and picture what is written on your tombstone. I told her I don't know because I have not seen it. She said I must know if I believe I am your killer. So, baby...what is it? What is written in stone?

Camille: What would you have written on her stone, Damon? What would you have said at her funeral?

Damon: I'm sorry. I'd say I'm sorry.

Camille: Elaborate. You dated this woman for two years and that's all you have to say?

Damon: What I have to say is irrelevant.

Camille: Irrelevant? Far from it. We are at the end of the world. Now is the best time as any other to speak what would be labeled unnecessary.

Damon: I wish I could see her one more time. I wish she had found her way back to me.

Camille: What would you have written?

I did not deserve an angel like you. From two separate worlds, two separate dreams. I wasted our time and I wasted your love. I took it all for granted as I have always done. In the last minutes of my life I hope my eyes close to a vision of your smile, your cuddly hug. A last warmth for the memory that I shattered. That I destroyed. If I pushed you into the arms of a killer, I regret it all. And if that killer was me, I will wake up soon to know it. To remember how you died. No man should think he killed a woman who bore so much love, but I feel a weight now that I never felt before, Anna. I feel like the bringer of death. Take this guilt from me and bury it with you.

Camille: Damon?

I clench my fists against my forehead.

Damon: You can't know these words. No one can.

51

Killer On The Road

Entry 51.

April 4th, 6:09 pm. I want to hold your diary in my own hands. Robbie carries the darn thing everywhere and re-reads passages just to see the pain in my eyes. He seems proud of himself, like he is the one who loved you so much, but you didn't really know him, did you? I hope he didn't hurt you. He is more sure than ever that I killed you out of spite to hide my sins, yet he is the one who carries weapons. Illegal blades tucked into the sides of his boots. Switchblades. Getting high so often doesn't help his mental state either. The man is primed for a kill.

"She was either oblivious to my being a bad boy or was just in a friendly mood when we chatted for the first time."

"Are you talking to yourself or me, Robbie?"

"Now I'm not sure. Have you ever been in a real fight, Flightplan?"

"My first wife Aleya. She threw a game console at my head."

"Did you retaliate?"

"I never hit back. I just ran outside to calm down."

"So it did upset you that she whacked you in the head."

"It hurt, Robbie. The projectile was dense."

"You cried."

"Not until she chased me down the street."

"Why did she do that?"

"To kiss me and tell me she was sorry."

"And did you accept the apology?"

"Yes."

"And you call yourself a killer. Ha Ha. I've handled knives during a hunt without flinching."

52

Campfire Fourwheel

Entry 52.

April 5th, 2:02 am. My aunt and uncle called me crazy for dumping you but they still loved me of course. They liked meeting you, Anna. I do wish we could go on one last ride down that trail by the waterfall. You giggled so much when I spun wheels through the mud banks. So cute.

I often have the same dream that wakes me up at night. You and me sitting in the back of my uncle's pickup on a trail driving back to the family cabin. We're surrounded by trees and the sun has set. The wind picks up and whips your red hair around your sweet face. You don't scoot closer to me, you just sit there smiling and blushing as I smile and wink back at you. I always wake up at the same part...your smile is fading when I start talking and I don't know what I am saying but suddenly tears fall down your cheeks and you turn to jump out of the truck bed. When I start to reach for your arm, my body jolts me awake.

And I start to cry on the airport floor. Because I will never see you again. I will never take you to the cabin again. We are nothing. We are gone.

53

Restricted

Entry 53.

April 6th, 3:23 pm. I did another painting in therapy. This time I stood with my back to the easel and Camille supervised as I moved the brush on the canvas with my hands behind my back. I was in literal handcuffs. Pink handcuffs. It was as hard as it sounds if not harder.

Camille: This is how you made Anna feel. Tied down. Trapped. Unable to be herself and create the way she wanted. You restricted her, Damon. You made her feel unloved and unable to satisfy.

Damon: I want to turn around and see the shit I'm drawing.

Camille: Not yet.

Damon: You didn't even let me pick the color.

Camille: You didn't let Anna pick her own outfits without your monstrously loud opinion about how awful they were.

Damon: I wasn't loud. I made a few grunts and heavy sighs when she walked out to the car but I didn't yell.

Camille: Arrogant pouting is worse. Why couldn't you just say she was beautiful to her face? Why couldn't you just tell her how much she meant to you without pointing out the flaws?

I feel the brush slip from my hand and Camille catches it before handing me a different one saturated with a different color.

Camille: Paint. Move.

Damon: I wanted credit for her confidence. I like when my women tell me I was right.

Camille: Anna was not yours. Aleya and Mishele weren't yours.

She yanks the brush from my fingers and pushes me to turn around. I see the paint on the canvas and I almost laugh. Only one lower corner is covered in toddler-like squiggles from my brushes.

Camille: You were forced to paint in handcuffs and you could only reach one spot on the canvas, Damon. You did that to your exes. You restricted their talents, their confidence. Relationships are not supposed to be a power trip for one king or queen.

She leaves me to fumble around on my own to free my wrists and yells at me as she opens a new bottle of red wine.

Camille: Relationships are a team. That's the point.

54

Ammunition

Entry 54.

April 7th, 1:12 pm. Robbie read another entry of yours to me today. It stung.

"You think a woman who is inexperienced is not capable of performing wifely duties."

"Well, yeah."

"Flightplan, that is dumb."

"She did have a lot to learn."

"And you didn't? She wrote in this page here that you had a stack of 'how to be a better husband' books in your dresser drawer. So clearly you never had it all figured out."

"No one has it figured out. Even after they are dead."

"**January 16th, 2019,**" Robbie read from your diary, "***I can't believe this is how it went down. I drive two and a half hours in traffic to pick you up from the airport, so excited to see you and welcome you home. I wait forty minutes near baggage claim before I see you come walking...you look so depressed, so miserable, we hug and I feel nothing from you. I see the distracted stare in your eyes the whole way driving back to your apartment. I don't exist anymore as your girlfriend. How did I know it was over then? You hadn't said a word.***"

He took a long look over the top of the pages to see my reaction. "That girl was on fire. Read it right before you read yourself."

I closed my laptop and stood up, chomped on the straw in my mouth. "More ammunition," I said through grit teeth.

Robbie watched me head toward the door. "Loving every minute of it."

55

Love Letters

Entry 55.

April 8th, 7:28 pm. I am a horrible speller and even worse at following the rules of grammar. I think it comes from a lack of concentration in school. But at least I can fix things, right? My mom also told me I was good at making people laugh. Humor always diffuses a spiny predicament.

"Did you ever put jokes in love letters?"

"What?" I looked over my shoulder at Richberg.

"Not talking to you, Scurts."

"He's talking to me," Garfrinks said. "I had a lot of girlfriends back in the day."

"You were a romantic or what?"

"I knew how to woo a lady." Blintz Garfrinks juggled shot glasses as he went on. "I was good with rhymes and I knew my flowers."

"Flowers?" I said.

"Hyacinth, gardenia, poppy, tiger flower."

"What's a tiger flower?" Richberg asked. He crumpled up several sheets of construction paper into a ball and licked it. "Since when are animals and flowers related?"

Garfrinks set each shot glass softly on the table. "You're dumb."

"Let me guess," I said. "The flowers have tiger stripes on the petals."

"Bright hues. Mostly orange from what I saw."

"You gave your girlfriends orange flowers?" Richberg sounded delirious as he chewed his paper. "Roses are the special ones."

I followed the nonsensical discussion while eating leftover popcorn that Lyrna had managed to pop by setting the bag outside on the runway in the afternoon heat. I thought about the diary entries Robbie had read to me, and then of one particular entry I got to read myself.

Anna's Diary: Inside jokes, long hugs before walking out the door, trying new restaurants, laughing until we cry, farting and burping contests. I don't miss my lover. I miss my best friend.

56

Abstract Wife

Entry 56.

April 9th, 3:45 pm. Admit it, baby. We pretended a lot. That it was all okay. That nothing was wrong. There were problems in our relationship from the start that neither one of us wanted to admit. They were red flags, warning sirens, yellow lights, stop signs...and we blew right past it all just to enjoy each other's company for a short and fast ride. You may not believe that I didn't mean to lead you on.

Camille: All she wanted was to love you and your family. She wanted to be a part of your family. That's what she wanted from you and all she got in return was insults to her body and personality.

Damon: I didn't expect them to be so mean to Anna.

Camille: Not behind her back, right?

Damon: I wasn't trying to be a jerk.

Camille: Did you talk about wedding plans with her?

Damon: I got excited sometimes thinking about our wedding day.

Camille: So you did imagine married life with her.

Damon: Yes.

Camille: What made you switch from wedding plans to cheating on her a week before dumping her?

Damon: I did not cheat on Anna. It was a clean break.

Camille: I can't picture you having a clean breakup, Damon. I picture you as the wishy-washy man going back for seconds with every girl you've been with.

Her lack of professionalism astounds me. I guess anything goes at the end of the world.

Damon: Lady, you weren't there.

There was no going back, Anna. When I let you go, I didn't think it would be forever. But I knew I could never turn back the clock. I lost seconds. I lost seconds with you and with everyone else. I never dropped down on one knee to propose to you because I didn't fall in love. I just liked pretending you were my wifey because you lit up every time I called you that. All I wanted was for you to smile and not be angry with me. I didn't want you to hate me.

57

Skydive

Entry 57.

April 10th, 12:43 pm. I read a passage from your diary. Robbie was scarfing a hamburger in front of me as I read it and hearing your voice in my head was a nice distraction from his savage chomping and constant spitting of dry bun crumbs onto the sticky table.

From Your Diary, Anna: We wish we could redo many things. But we can't. It's impossible to rewind. Yet we try. We try to make "settling" and "good enough" work. And why do I think my story is worth telling? Because in the complexities of life, every single one of us on the planet has a story to share. And from what I have learned, this adventure of life wouldn't be the same without all the bumps in the road.

Falling out of a plane strapped to an instructor does add up to something. I have three points to my Theory Of Skydive and why it is relevant to a healthy mind.

First of all, the minute after you watch the inspirational instructional video with old school guitar shredding in the background, you find your-self hesitating before signing the line on the form that says in other words "we are not responsible for your death or injuries..." And though this makes your heart thump faster, you do it anyway because heck, it's time

to live!

Second, there is this sense of bravery as you board the plane together with other tandem jumpers and a few solo skydivers. It's the kind of feeling where you know you are about to do something kinda stupid but incredibly cool and you know you better enjoy every second of it in case you really end up going splat. The thought of dying instead of landing safe pops into your head several times on the way up so you keep up your smiling for the camera even if it is just for a last picture.

Third, the door opens and your instructor scoots you both toward the exit. This is the part in which you know you have to trust this stranger you just met with your life, and wussing out is not an option for a doer like you. When you see others ahead of you just drop over the edge and be taken by the sky, it looks insane. It looked like a cinematic dream to me as I inched closer to the edge with my instructor. Your mind literally goes blank realizing what you are about to do. He had one hand on the plane and I heard the words barely in the wind: "You ready?"

I thought no way but I screamed yes and we were gone out of the plane and the first five seconds my stomach dropped as he back-flipped. I remember later thinking and re-watching the video...wow. Really? Take a newbie up and show off with that kind of maneuver? Okay. Ha. Ha.

The rest of the fall - fall, not jump - was a strange feeling. Wind is blasting around freezing your ears and you almost feel like you are driving with the top down during a super windy day at the beach. But it is louder than that and it truly is like being a flying superhero. You know you are going down but freefall to me felt more like a horizontal flight with arms and legs positioned as instructed.

Then the parachute snaps open and you float down in the loudest silence you could hear. It is stunning.

I read that out loud, Anna. I'm so proud you, baby. You're braver than me. You're better. You're stronger. And I envy you.

"You are so stupid to let that unicorn go," Robbie said to me. "She was incredible." He snatched the diary back across the table before I could hug it to my chest. "Ah ah. Still mine."

"You didn't date her."

"And," he said into his glass of peach ice tea, "I didn't break her heart."

58

Drunk Text

Entry 58.

April 11th, 10:02 pm. You know what my favorite drink is? Screwdriver. So good. Sooooo refreshing. Also the Eastern European ladies like laughing with me as I try to speak their languages. It's weird being locked up in an airport with so much alcohol flowing...you'd think the government wouldn't want us homeless types to have access to all the untouched bars but I keep going back to what I call the booze hall and sit under dusty counters with bottles in hand. One hand on my laptop and the other around the neck of pure vodka. Remember that one time I texted you when I was on that layover? You told me I sounded drunk. How do you read a drunk text? How do you interpret one?

"Scurts, what's that?"

"Huh?"

"Backpack. Vodka bottles. Where you get that?"

"What do you mean? The booze hall's got all this shit strewn everywhere. Am I the only one who knows of it?"

Richberg traded lofted eyebrows with Garfrinks. "None of us drink much."

I had to smile. "Anna never drank much either. She got drunk once...I had forgotten that incident until Robbie read the entry she wrote about that night."

Anna's Diary: I kept running in circles with the bottle hoping to Heaven that you wouldn't take it away from me. I didn't want our vacation to end...preferring the idea of Sasquatch catching and eating me than having to drive back to the airport in the morning. I felt free with you and your family in the Maryland forest. Romantic and memory-making. You ignored me through so much of the trip so I cried that night. I drank almost the whole wine bottle and I was proud of it when you finally caught up to me laying upside down on the cabin's living room couch. I giggled like a maniac and I wept because I knew somehow that you were finished with me.

59

Side Chicks

Entry 59.

April 12th, 4:44 pm. Camille says you were just being a rational woman in the circumstances...any woman would be hurt to discover the truth, she said. I don't think I was wrong. I did my best.

Camille: What makes a woman crazy, Damon?

Damon: I don't know.

Camille: Being second place makes her crazy. Being lied to makes her crazy. Flirting with other women in front of her makes her crazy. Using her as a side chick when you have a new girlfriend? That makes her insane.

Damon: If she wasn't so sensitive, she would never have lost her mind.

Camille: Not every woman wants to keep a lid on their emotions. You can't force a passionate soul into a silent box and expect her to stay there. Did your ex-wives have breaking points? Did they ever snap?

Damon: Aleya snapped all the time. She was a wild filly day and night.

Camille: And you were married to her for six years.

Damon: I was.

Camille: And Mishele? Did she snap?

Damon: No. She was level-headed. Even when she wanted a divorce after ten years, she and I worked it out in the calmest way.

Camille: That's not normal. What aren't you telling me about them?

Damon: There is nothing else to know.

Camille: Did you have side chicks when you were married to either of them?

Damon: When I got bored I talked to cute girls online.

Camille: While married?

The judgment in her eyes scorns every part of my body.

Damon: My morals are not yours.

Camille: Nothing close, Mr. Scurto. Nothing close to my idea of commitment and making vows.

Damon: No one says I have to wear a wedding ring to prove my love.

Camille: Symbolism is not a suggestion. It's proof. How can you love anyone in a genuine manner if you label them all with a number? If you see me as a 5 or Aleya as a 10 or a random woman on the street as a 2...if you see us all as numbers, are we not all side chicks? Are we not all pawns in your game of catch and release? Short term pleasure? You burned all of them and you escaped unscathed.

I don't want to respond. I don't want to raise my voice at her.

Damon: They gave me nightmares. Anna gave me guilt. I spent all those years of my life feeling nothing but pleasure and love for beautiful women and here I am.

I hold out my arms, my laptop on the floor right next to my feet. Sweat is dripping down my glasses.

Damon: I'm not unscathed, lady. Look at my scars.

Her voice comes out as a whisper. She pours herself more red wine.

Camille: I see a narcissist.

60

Ego

Entry 60.

April 13th, 1:09 pm. I never considered myself a mean person or even cold. I know how to cry. Whenever I did cry in front of you I felt like I was losing control of my body...every sob brought me closer to leaning on your shoulder and you would rub my back with the gentlest of touches. You knew how to break a man's ego. And I had one of the biggest egos around. I knew it. I still do.

"Did you always walk ahead of her?"

"No."

"You never held her hand in public either according to her diary. She kept a picture she took of an airport terminal with you walking way ahead of her. You never wanted to be viewed as a couple."

"Not true. I enjoyed her company."

"You like your freedom," Robbie said around a bite of fish stick.

"Who doesn't?"

"My Marga gave me plenty of space but we still held hands in public. I liked trailing back to see her cute butt once in a while, but other than that I liked being right with her."

"Did you plan on marrying her?"

"I wanted to but she didn't." Robbie sniffed the rim of his beer bottle. "Marga kept saying she needed more time to think about us."

"And?"

He played with both forks on the plate, pushing pieces of fry and fish in circles.

"I don't know, Flightplan. I always wanted to have a family, like the wife and kids thing. Hurts when they say no. Bruises the ego."

"My therapist would say I have an ego bigger than yours."

Robbie smirked. "Narcissists always have the bigger ego."

61

Pedestal

Entry 61.

April 14th, 9:53pm. Any woman who gives great back massages and cooks for hours in the kitchen while I game is a gem in my book. Problem is that mindset has led me to deliver many heartbreaks when a good woman doesn't deliver on my expectations. Sounds stupid, and as Robbie said, I probably should be thankful that no girls tried hunting me down after what I did to all of them.

"Stupid is as stupid does, Scurts."

"Thanks, Richberg. I really needed to hear that."

"We both know there was never a pedestal. You wanted them to worship you and your needs. It feels amazing to be adored by a beautiful woman until they snap out of the trance and realize they are being played."

"So you played your wife?"

"I didn't. I was a king from day one, not a snake like you."

I shrugged, glancing at our shadows on the hard floor. The flames from outside illuminated parts of the terminal that were usually pitch black. Every bit of the smooth hard floor glowed orange under our feet as we paced in the late hour.

"If I agree that I am a snake does that make me a better person?"

Richberg half-grinned. "No. But at least you agree."

"If," I said back to him. "If I agree."

"The less you admit, Scurts, the more it will hurt inside."

"I did not stand on a pedestal."

He shook his head as he ripped a piece of green paper to chew. "That's all you stand on, Scurts. Your women never got the praise they deserved. You got it all."

62

Too Late

Entry 62.

April 15th, 2:31 am. I know you hate apologies. You screamed at me even after I texted sorry a hundred times. Look, if I knew how this would end, I would've never emailed you my number. I just wanted to give you a chance, babe. I just wanted to have fun. I never took our trips as seriously as you did, Anna. I thought you were casual too. I thought it was all for fun while you kept me company. I hated being alone.

63

Lake Cabin

Entry 63.

April 16th, 1:22 pm. Remember the overlook at Scumeklhie's Rock? You told me you felt something electric up there with my arms around you, squeezing your body against mine. The gentle kiss I placed on your cheek as we looked out at the Yogerli River. Two souls never meant to be but meant to be together two years at a time. It feels like it should never have happened...like our paths should have never crossed.

"She respected you in the beginning, Flightplan. Wouldn't be too off to say she was head over heels from the first day you went out."

I pushed the empty glass to the edge of the table and went to work sipping the second milkshake. "I thought she was cool too."

"No, you didn't. You thought she was a dork from day one."

"I liked it."

"You played her. Why don't you just admit that?"

"That week I took her to the cabin, Robbie. I had feelings for her then."

"Yeah, and yet four months later you cheated."

"I did not cheat."

"You overlapped."

"No. I met the next one after Anna drove away."

"Wow wow wow. The lies. Tell me how this makes sense then. In her diary she wrote that whenever you went out to dinner you would joke about having a double date years later with a new girlfriend for you and a new boyfriend for her. She was hurt by that. You were telling her without telling her that you wanted to break up."

"I don't need to be direct."

"How is that not lying?"

Fine, Anna. I lied. I lied all the time.

64

The Steak

Entry 64.

April 17th, 7:59 pm. I heard this funny story once about a guy who owned my favorite restaurant. Apparently, he started it as a dare with his dad because they were going to prove his uptight stepmom wrong about their ability to cook in the kitchen. Sounds kinda stupid but it's funny because they made it huge and his stepmom never complained or came around again...of course it's sad that she was the second chick to leave his dad in eight months.

"I miss dinner dates. My wife and I went to a place where the owners greeted us all the time." Richberg sat facing the windows, hands empty of paper this time. "It was far from romantic."

"What was it called?"

"Burnt Squarez."

"What the heck was that?"

"Mostly burnt chicken and crispy peanut butter cookies."

"They served that on one plate?" I said. "And you ate it?"

"What's weird is they never gave us proper hydration for it. Had to bring bottled water from the shop across the street."

"You and your wife chose that over steak?"

"Since when is steak the better dinner option for a date, Scurts? Are you not adventurous?"

"Not really," I said.

"Looking at your pudgy middle, I can imagine how many steaks and fries you had in your lifetime."

I glanced down at myself. "Sure, Richberg. Least I can live off my fat if we run out of food in the last few weeks."

Anna, you know I liked my routine even though you thought it was boring. It's nice to know what comes next. Surprises were never my thrill. I know I'm boring.

65

Forgiveness

Entry 65.

April 18th, 12:55 am. I was never an empathetic person. I don't love the way you did, babe. I guess loving deeply and truly is something I never saw in my world...until you did your darndest to show me what a passionate heart looked like. You forgave me in our relationship over and over when I caused you hurt. You forgave me then. I wonder if you would forgive me now...if you had ever let go of the anger.

66

One Hundred Five Miles

Entry 66.

April 19th, 1:33 pm. One hundred five miles. That's how much you drove one way. A four hour round trip every other weekend for two years. That's how much you loved me. I never loved as much as you, Anna. I never truly loved at all.

"One hundred five. That's the hottest day I spent sitting in a jail cell."

"When's the last time you were behind bars?"

"I was pardoned in 2032. Only a few years ago when all this hell began cascading down into the cities. I was told that I no longer had a dangerous reputation and that I could walk free on the street." He lifted his wrist and I held up mine. "Once I got the mandated bracelet, of course. Brothers in oblivion, Flightplan."

"I imagined oblivion to be colder. More like outer space than this daily microwave."

"Oblivion means mortality in my world. Absolute certainty of death. The reasons for living on are few."

"What keeps you here, Robbie?"

"Honestly?" He took the diary and laid it gently on the table between us. We waited for our lunch brought by Miss Cuteness before Robbie spoke again. "Anna's words. Her words have cracked me up and made me feel all the emotion I lost in prison. I still think you were an idiot for letting her go. But in another way, it seems she was the lucky one to be severed from your path."

I leaned over the table, stabbing a piece of watery coleslaw and sipping a flat soda at the same time. "She's lucky to have gone through the pain I put her in and then be killed by a crazy human? Specifically killed by you or me?" I waved my fork up at him. "Tell me."

Robbie looked ready to tell a long and intense tale as he breathed in deep and stretched both arms out before tucking them back at his sides. "You take credit for way too much of Anna's interests, Flightplan. What makes you think you influenced her to like everything that you did?"

"I got her into fast cars, dogs, military aircraft and tanks, guns, dark chocolate..."

"False!" Robbie shouted at me. He held up all ten fingers. "She loved fast cars before you met her. She grew up with and properly loved more dogs than you ever did. She had always respected the military and loved war history from her first day in high school. And dark chocolate is just nasty." He scowled into his rum-laced milkshake. "No one likes that."

I smirked while holding my cup in the air. "Your point?"

"Anna called you a lost soul." He smiled as he said it, pride punctuated into every word.

"Sometimes, Robbie," I said. "We can't all outrun the dark."

One hundred five miles. That's how much you loved me.

67

Soldier's Face

Entry 67.

April 20th, 1:46 am. War is not how we picture it in the movies. With every hour spent watching a WW2 documentary on the couch, laying my head in your lap, there came the pleasures of laziness and contentment. I never had the fear of being called to go fight and leave what I loved. I was never called to step up in an act of what you would call 'crazy stupid courage'. I wasn't born to defend land or humanity, babe. My face is round, my eyesight has worsened, I have no scars that tell a heroic story.

Your eyes always locked on the faces of the soldiers in movies. I saw how you lit up watching them fight until the end and you probably wished it was me leading a charge across a field. You wished I had a soldier's face and a warrior's heart. I don't. I like my comforts, I enjoyed being pampered by both my ex-wives. I disappointed you and I didn't really care to change my efforts. We don't change at our core. I have never changed. I have always been Damon R Scurto. Not a soldier. Not a hero. Just an attention-starved boy in the body of an aging man.

68

Mountains

Entry 68.

April 21st, 3:29 pm. Have you ever heard such a silence as the wind in the night sky? The higher the elevation, the quieter it remains. I still prefer the mountains to the beach. I never gave up the framed pictures I got for my apartment all those years ago. I brought them everywhere I moved until the day of the nuclear attack. I just stared at the mountaintops in the snowy cabin painting, sitting on the edge of my bed, wishing for a teleportation switch. That was my position, taken right before the ceiling collapsed and the windows shattered within half a second.

Camille: You're lucky to be alive.

I sit against a trash bin, face to the windows.

Damon: I don't need you to tell me that. I know my luck.

Camille: You think your luck has run out.

Damon: I feel like death is coming.

Camille: Death is coming for all of us. Not just you, Damon. I feel the same. The shortened hours of my internal clock.

Damon: We will not survive the next strike.

Camille: No. We will not.

She sighs and sets down her pen. Her tipsy eyes fix on the horizon outside the windows.

Camille: Are you afraid of death?

I say nothing more to her. Close my eyes and dream of mountains.

Anna, if you were alive, would you have answered the knock at your door?

If I had come to your lake house, would you have let me in for one more hug?

69

Mama's Boy

Entry 69.

April 22nd, 1:21 pm. I'm supposed to protect my family. I'm supposed to be their golden child if I am their only child. A burden I know, Anna. I always picked fights about girls I brought home and I always stood on the line between you and my mama. Unfortunately, she always won. I did everything to please her.

"I never knew my mom. I was in foster care most of my years as a kid."

Robbie spat out a piece of soggy bread onto the pavement. We sat outside of the diner with our backs against the front door squinting against the sun.

"What was that like?" I asked.

"Not very great. But I was my own parent when there weren't any around. I was responsible for myself."

"So you turned into a criminal."

"That was not my plan." Robbie's eyes were angry. "I never wanted to be who I am now."

"But you chose it the same way I chose to break Anna's heart."

"And you think you made the right choice?"

"My family knew she wasn't right for me. My mom argued with me about being with a better woman."

Robbie took off his glasses to rub his nose. "Whose opinion mattered more, Flightplan?"

"I wanted Anna to be happy and I wanted my mom to be happy."

"Care to share the logic in your actions? You have hurt everyone around you. No one ended up happy."

"I just tried to make them proud."

"Proud of what? You wanted a mommy as your wife and Mishele provided that. She filled the gap that Anna couldn't. Wasn't that why you married her?"

"In the moment it was smart."

"It was a joke. Why would any man marry his mother?"

I looked away as I put a cigarette to my mouth. "I hate doing laundry."

"Beauty as a servant," Robbie said in a whisper. "Wicked genius."

I'm not a bad guy, Anna. I'm not.

70

Pleasure

Entry 70.

April 23rd, 2:08 am. Nobody tells us that happiness is short-lived in a relationship. It just takes a dive at the wrong time. It's the same for all people. We desire the passion, the excitement in every moment of the day. What's impossible is sustaining it for a lifetime. I admit I'm addicted to pleasure. I'm addicted to the thrills that come from fast cars, hotel overnights, flirty waitresses, making love in an unsavory place. It gives me purpose and pride for the moment. And that moment dissipates as a firework doused by rain. Pleasure is the invisible demon. It always comes and always leaves.

We are warned of the pain that will follow, but we never listen. No one, young or old, does. It's a trap. Pleasure is always a trap.

71

Are You Happy?

Entry 71.

April 24th, 4:12 pm. Resilience is a rare quality. You were the most resilient person I had ever met. Not to mention, Anna, you were a giggly creature. You knew how to enjoy any small moment of humor, no matter how juvenile it was. You could make me smile even when I was at my most anxious and I thank you for that gift. Laughter is what I crave most outside intimacy.

Camille: Are you ever happy now?

Damon: Not exactly. You might call it content to be discontent.

Camille: That is not the point to life.

Damon: Then what is? Why the hell am I even talking to you about any of my problems?

Camille: Your impatience with me stems from a desire to be glorified, Mr. Scurto. All you ever want is attention from beautiful people. It's nice to be liked, isn't it? It's nice to be adored.

I chew my lip as I pace the floor. The smell of rum and vanilla hovers between me and the glass.

Damon: When did you start drinking the rum?

Camille: Every cabinet is smashed in the booze hall. I take what I want when I want, and besides that, my wine is all gone.

Damon: A therapist can't cure someone of guilt if they are guilty themselves.

Camille: I am not guilty of murder, Mr. Scurto.

I stare hard at her.

Damon: Call me Damon.

Camille: You told me about the other entries she wrote in her diary. You told me what she said.

Anna's Diary: That day. I was scared of you, Damon. The look in your eyes when you grabbed me, pushed me. I said nothing to provoke it. I said nothing to stop it. You saw my eyes fill with tears and yet you pushed me hard against the sink. What is wrong with you?

Damon: I was not myself, Camille. My mind was not in a forgiving place.

Camille: What did she do to make you respond like that?

I reach for the pack of cigarettes on her fold-up desk and stick one in my mouth.

Damon: She scraped up the side of my car.

72

Unfinished

Entry 72.

April 25th, 11:04 am. I didn't know you were in the ground until I tried to set up one last visit. I thought about you throughout my second marriage, Anna. About what could've been. I always wanted to see you one last time even though you told me that would never happen. You said to stay with the new woman and not chase after you. You said you are not a trophy, not a mistress. But I still haven't forgotten what you did for me.

"She talked in her sleep."

I saw a piece of rubbery cheese slip out between the bread as I looked at Robbie. "What?"

"Yeah." He licked the edges of the greasy paper plate. "Sometimes she talked about you."

"No way. You weren't there."

He was smirking. "Pretty sure. Yeah, I was there."

"You watched her sleep in her room?"

"Nah, just outside the window at the foot of her bed."

"How many women have you stalked?"

Robbie shrugged and let out a casual hum as he delicately sipped orange juice. "Only ten or twelve. Anna was a favorite though. I still liked her when I was with my Marga."

"You stalked twelve women?"

"Ten or twelve. And I would track down your ex Aleya to join that party but she said on the phone that she is so far off the grid we might as well call her dead and buried."

"You told Aleya that you're a stalker?"

"Mhm. She's cool. We're at the end of the world anyway." He raised the clear plastic cup and waved it back and forth. "More orange drink, Cuteness!"

"Robbie, you just notched yourself up to a new level of crazy."

"So what? You don't like women to be crazy so I want to honor them with my being crazy too." He poured the bottom half of a beer bottle into his cup to mix it with the orange juice. "It's called being supportive."

I glowered.

"And also being sane is boring. Who has time for snobby cold shoulders when the life of the party is always the dorky idiosyncratic one writing fantasy poetry in the corner?"

"No one likes the dorky one at the party, Rob."

"Anna was dorky. You hated it because she cramped your style."

"I had an image to build."

"Yeah." Robbie was nose-deep in his drink. "A crappy one."

73

Broken

Entry 73.

April 26th, 1:34 am. Richberg and Garfrinks are kicking a soccer ball down the booze hall again. The bobby-bangs lady is just talking to herself on the luggage carousel. I can't sleep because of the nightmares. The guilt is weighing me down more than ever as I stare out at the skyline. I don't remember getting violent with you, Anna. I don't remember attacking you in any way. Yet there are dreams...dreams of me standing over your grave and smiling about it. How could that be me? How could I smile at your death? I keep seeing your grave and I jolt up every time covered in sweat and gasping like I had just resurfaced from a deep ocean dive.

I feel like I am broken inside, like my body is breaking apart slowly as I search for the truth of my pain and where you are. Did I send you into the arms of a killer? Am I that killer? Did I do this?

74

I Am

Entry 74.

April 27th, 4:15 pm. I am sorry. I know it does not mean anything to you. I know seeing you one last time would've been a mistake. But dammit all I've made are mistakes and the biggest one was leaving you. If crawling back is a mistake, then let it be. I never meant to break your heart.

Camille: Are you sure you never had cruel intentions?

Damon: I am not a bad guy.

Camille: How do you know that? You trust yourself?

Damon: I'm not sure of anything. I just feel darkness welling up in me all the time.

Every time I stand on the runway, I think about going home. I know my return would only be met with grief. Nothing is the same or will ever be the same again. The reality of time and what it does to the heart is bruising. You can forget many hurts, but if all we do is live in the moment then we will miss out on the deepness that comes later. Pain will come when we sweep current consequences under the rug. Pain always comes back around. No matter how good you think you've been, it strikes you.

Camille: I don't trust your honesty.

Damon: I hear that a lot.

Camille: Do you think you have faced consequences?
Damon: I am the consequences. I am living them right now.

75

Keep It

Entry 75.

April 28th, 12:17 pm. Robbie has become more than a best friend. He is also one of the meanest people I've had the pleasure to meet. I tell him to keep his insults to himself but he lets them rip all the time. He seems smitten with a dead woman and, frankly, I don't blame him. The woman who wrote that diary is something special, Anna. You were. You are.

"Did you see the look in her eyes before you killed her?"

"No. I mean I don't remember. But the guilt is real."

"You said you killed her. You said you think you did."

"I think I'm just as criminal as you, Robbie."

"What do you know for sure? Did you ever have the urge for blood?"

"Not that I can remember."

"So all of this could be under fabricated memories. Are you prepared to be wrong, Flightplan?"

"I did something to put her in danger. I know I did. She died and I feel like her death is on my conscience. I just don't know why or how."

"I have an entry here that may refresh your memory. Listen."

Anna's Diary: I have never been a fan of freeway driving but I was thrilled to drive you back from the airport, babe. I was so happy when

you fell asleep in shotgun, totally trusting me to drive the two hours home. It was great until you woke up and pointed out that I should speed up a bit in the next lane over. I was already going 75, Damon. You know I hate going any faster than that and then there was the rain. You critique the way I hold the steering wheel and the way I do my lane changes. I wish you had just shut up and gone back to sleep so I could comfortably drive my way.

"You did have quite the temper. She was scared of you."

"I never hit her."

"You were a massive critic about everything she did. It says it right here, Flightplan."

"I had a breaking point."

"Over a car? She was driving and you got to relax after she picked you up from the airport. Sounds like you had it made."

"She drove like a maniac!"

Robbie grinned at my outburst. He slid the diary toward me and gestured to it. "Read the rest."

My face burned as I slammed my laptop closed. "Keep it," I said. I shook my head hard. "Keep the dang book. She was a maniac."

"So were you."

Anna's Diary: You got rough with me last night...shoving me against the closet door. What gives you the right to gloat about your exes when I'm standing right in front of you? You walked me past the jewelry store in the mall three times yesterday talking about engagement rings and you're telling me you miss Aleya's perfect body?

Robbie chuckled as he closed the diary. "You have a seed of cruelty in you, Flightplan. This entry is one of many that proves it."

"What set me off that day?"

"Indeed."

"I think I was drunk, Robbie. No, I was defending Aleya because Anna was trash-talking her."

"Fighting dirty as usual. You know you can't fantasize about a hot ex in front your girlfriend. That's the messiest tactic there is."

"Anna was hot too. I never said she wasn't."

Robbie switched the cigarette in his left hand to his right before calmly pouring vodka in both our shot glasses. "Appearances should never count in the end, Flightplan. But yes, I agree she was very hot."

He raised his glass and I raised mine.

76

Night Terror

Entry 76.

April 29th, 4:21 am. I have nightmares because of you, because of what I've done. Robbie said in your diary you said you had worse dreams than mine. He thinks it's funny that I have bad dreams now. Calls it karma when I wake up screaming on the sticky airport floor. Hell, the man is mean.

This is the first time we spent the entire night with no power. No light sources. No charging outlets. No hum of vending machines. If this is how they are planning on killing us...slow and silent...they will do a great job. I keep hearing Richberg hacking in the dark next to me. Then a rip of paper as he prepares to chew another piece. Lyrna is crunching her crackers several feet away. The slightest noises are amplified in the pitch black dark. Every little whisper and echo keeps my eyes open. Sleep barely comes.

The sounds outside the terminal are the worst. Hum of the electric wires two inches from the door, crackling of the gunfire spouting from the government vehicles aiming at stragglers on the streets, the sirens being tested over and over for another nuclear strike.

77

Window Seat

Entry 77.

April 30th, 11:31 am. Not only did Robbie have the means to fly me to the gravesite but he brought your diary on board and I had yet to hold it in my own hands. Strange they let people like us on one of the last passenger jets. All we have is the regular civilian bracelet. Nothing special. No sign of pathetic valor or glorified treason.

"How long has it been since you been on a flight, Scurto?"

"As passenger or pilot?"

"Both."

"I don't remember."

"Your memory just getting worse or you that dumb?"

"I don't know what's happening to my head, Robbie. Stop being an ass."

"You're aging so horrible, my man."

"You say that too much. Mishele thought I was adorable. So did Aleya."

"And you say that too much, Flightplan. Stop being an ass. We're here for Anna, right? Isn't that why we're on this plane? For Anna?"

"Yes," I mumbled. "For Anna."

"What if I told you I had been there from the beginning...if I said I had seen her in her first relationship. Year 2010. I was there on her campus."

"And?"

"I was in an astronomy class with her. I sat three rows back watching her every move."

"Did she ever notice you?"

"No, she was occupied with her love interest back then."

"You were secretly desiring her company that whole time?"

Robbie looked out the window at the clear air around the wing. "It wasn't about her company."

"What did you want?"

"I wanted what any man wants. For her to want me."

This is sounding twisted, Anna. Did you have any love for this man? Any meaningful connection? Or is it just the alcohol surging in his veins?

"When did you see her next?"

"Off and on for years, Flightplan. By the time you two broke up I was there to be her support and she had no clue she needed any crutches. I got her into night running after we met on the sidewalk next to her mailbox."

"Night running? And she wasn't afraid to run in the dark?"

"I was right there. I protected her when we went down the path."

"How long did you run with her?"

Robbie unclicked his seatbelt and started to stand up. "Bathroom." He looked down at me. "Long as it took for her to release her anger. You really did a number on her, Flightplan. I was her confidant."

78

Following Robbie

Entry 78.

May 1st, 4:41 pm. This new airport smells different, the carpet under my bare feet feels different, the sounds echoing through the terminal are stranger than before. Robbie is looking for food while I sit here typing and I can't believe how wild he has become. He's using knives to stab through old luggage and throwing bricks at airport store windows. I can smell his adrenaline and suddenly I fear him.

It is futile to grow anything in the fibers of a standard commercial carpet and yet the homeless people in this airport have laid out piles of dirt in an attempt to create a garden. The soil is glistening from a recent watering and is now smeared into thin patches as Robbie stomps through it.

"I'm an animal," he mutters as he walks past where I sit. "Nowhere to run. Nowhere to die."

I closed my laptop and clutched it in my arms as I sat on the floor.

"We are forgotten," I said to Robbie.

He lifted his left arm weakly above his head as he shuffled toward the broken escalator. Half a cigarette was perched between his index and middle fingers. Robbie was exactly how I imagined a wayward, broken man to be...eating unhealthy food all the time but as skinny as a birch tree, cough-guffawing and then gazing into space at spontaneous intervals, no regard for onlookers when he was in the middle of a rant. An appearance of madness and my own absolute certainty that I was beginning to look the same way to outsiders.

79

Shadows Of Steps

Entry 79.

May 2nd, 1:53 am. Robbie Decker is telling me things that a person could know only if they lived in my brain or were breathing down my neck day and night. I swear he is more alien than human, maybe even supernatural like the witches in the 90s horror films my mama loved to joke about. If a person can really be possessed, maybe he is one of those people. Should I be ready to defend myself from a darker power?

80

No Light

Entry 80.

May 3rd, 7:14 pm. I am afraid to leave this new airport. I don't know this landscape outside. I don't remember it. There is no time to make friends with the homeless group relegated to this place, but I doubt they would be any nicer than the paper-eating, cracker-munching, block-building crew back at my west wind airport. I only know the name of one person here in this terminal. The man paces the last remaining jet bridge dressed in a blue sweater with cut-off sleeves and torn office slacks. He goes barefoot like Richberg did. He told me to call him Jenack.

"How long you here for?"

"Only til Robbie takes me to the grave."

"Why did you come so far just to see a dead woman?"

I didn't respond.

"What was her name?"

"Anna."

"Did you love her?"

"Only after I found she was gone."

"You came all this way for a pile of dirt, son."

"I know," I said.

"Messed up, ya know. I never had a true love."

I followed him as he walked to the edge of the jet bridge. "My true loves left me."

"Then why go anywhere for a love that never was?"

"I feel guilty."

He took a stick of gum from his pocket. "Closure, right?"

"Yeah."

Orange smoke rolled in across the runway outside.

"Closure's for fools," Jenack said. "It's not real."

"It has to help me. I can't have one night without a bad dream?"

"Thou doth not suffer alone," he said, and walked away.

Closure is justice. If I'm wrong, Anna, then I hope I die like you.

81

Death Sentence

Entry 81.

May 4th, 7:33 pm. I don't know how it will happen to me. I once assumed of natural causes. For all I know at this point Robbie Decker might be the one who chokes me out with one of his shoelaces. He is just as angry at me as you were. I don't know if it's the way he is protecting you with his jealousy or if it's just him being upset that a guy like me ruined all good men's chances. He's becoming erratic...probably because he's high.

"I did kill people, but I had a reason to," Robbie said as we blew smoke into the rusty sky. "You were just a selfish butthead."

"Really? Butthead?"

"What kind of boyfriend kills the best woman he ever had?"

"Maybe I was jealous."

"Jealous?" He coughed and rolled over laughing. "Jealousy ain't your problem, Flightpan."

"Should I be running for my life?"

"I'm the least of your worries, you murderer." He sat up again, spit out a piece of gum, put the cigarette to his mouth.

"So you do know I killed her."

"You're mean, Flightplan. And I...I'm a different kind of evil."

"Evil?"

"You don't expect what I can do."

"What do I expect, Robbie?"

He ripped the cigarette from my mouth and grabbed my face in his hands, shaking me without saying anything until, "I'm capable." He fell over laughing and kept laughing like a maniac for the rest of the night.

82

Old Age

Entry 82.

May 5th, 6:55 pm. No one wants their last days to be in the midst of evil. I watch soldiers load planes outside the airport windows and I wonder what is to become of us inside. The last of the aircraft is to be moved, and the airport? By order of the governing law, we are to be demolished with it. Our lives don't matter anymore. I miss my old friends, my old life. I miss how the world was when you were in it. I miss having hope.

"Sucks getting old, doesn't it?" Jenack said. He was sitting on the check-in counter with a bowl of microwaved rice. "Can't get comfortable day or night with the arthritis."

"Don't have that yet," I replied.

"Can't wait to get to Heaven once this world is over."

"You're a Christian?"

"I am, but I don't dress myself in crosses and robes."

"I don't either."

"You know you're going up there too?"

"I hope."

"You better have someone pray for your soul, bud."

"How old are you, Jenack?"

"Seventy-seven. I've lived a life or two."

"Will you pray for me?"

He paused with his spoon in the air and a piece of rice dropped from it. He said nothing and then gave a slow nod before spooning the rice into his mouth.

"Thank you," I said.

83

Anna

Entry 83.

May 6th, 3:13 am. Anna, this is for you. For whatever it's worth, for whatever pain I caused, I hope you did forgive me in your final moments. I wish we could have shared one last kiss or at least a warm embrace. I'm not a bad guy, or I try not to be bad. Maybe I killed you, maybe it was an accident. I never wanted to find you this way.

I never forgot you. I never forgot the dorky 80s dance moves in the middle of my living room, the midnight giggle attacks you had after I farted, the way you shrieked and jumped up and down in anger when I said I deleted your saved game and then the look of shock when I laughed and revealed I was teasing, the way you got tipsy and super loopy after one wine cooler, the back massages that put me to sleep after just fifteen minutes of your amazing hands, the blushing smile you tried to hide whenever I winked at you...I will never forget any part of you, Anna.

I remember enough of our time to make me sad and to make me miss what cannot be taken back. Every gesture of love you gave freely, every hour you spent driving in the dark alone on the long freeway, every minute cuddling under a blanket with you in front of a stupidly funny movie, every kiss that you gave and never demanded from me. You were as unselfish as they come, baby, and I owe you. I owe you everything.

84

I Did Nothing

Entry 84.

May 7th, 7:11 pm. I watched you stand there and cry. You shuddered, you dropped to your knees, you held your hands over your face while snotty tears cascaded everywhere. In the last hour we were drifting further from each other than we ever had ever before, and that time it was a cold break for me. I had already moved on and I was watching you fly away. Watching my angel fly away. Doing nothing to stop it.

"It's hard to let the good ones go," Jenack had said. "But we relinquish that which we do not want. And you never wanted her."

I felt faint next to Robbie. We stood in the intersection across from the cemetery.

"Better to die standing in the fight than on your knees as a coward," Richberg had once said.

Robbie crossed the street and I waited ten seconds before following.

"I'd rather you do nothing now," Lyrna had said, "than pretend to be brave for a dead person."

I am not a hero. I am not a warrior.

"We're here, Flightplan." Robbie's arm was outstretched in front of me. "That one."

My boots felt like they were being sucked into the dirt as I came forward.

"I did nothing for her," I whispered.

"For you," Robbie said behind me. "She lived for you."

85

Speak To The Grave

Entry 85.

May 7th, 8:48 pm. Robbie finally gave me your diary, baby. He dropped it on your grave right in front of my feet. I should've been happy but the gesture scared me. I knew there would be one final payment.

"You act like you could reverse a broken heart or even death. That would be quite the gift indeed."

"There doesn't have to be an end to anything. Not my life or hers."

"But Anna is dead. You can't take that back. You can't dig up the grave and bring her back with a kiss, Damon."

"I know."

"So?"

"So I dream. I dream of it."

"Who does that help?" He circled me. "How has that helped?"

"It makes me feel better."

"You mean it makes you feel less like shit."

"Guilty."

He stood behind me as I stared down at the dirt. "So," he said. "Are you ready to die for the woman you killed?"

I heard a click before my mouth opened, and at the second I swiveled my head, I felt the gun at the base of my neck. "No. I didn't...I didn't."

"She wasn't afraid of death." He shoved it into my shoulder blade until I dropped to my knees. "You are." Robbie's words hissed against my ear. "She never saw it coming, Flightplan. Anna sought solace in the company of grieving shadows and so did I. I'm not a fan of torture but I told you I never waste a person's time."

"So you killed her."

"I acted on impulsion. I never lie."

I'm sorry, baby. I should've protected you. "I didn't kill Anna."

"You are nothing like me. No guts, no passion, no reason for falling in love. At least..." Robbie faltered, took the gun away from my neck. "I was honest. I can live with that."

Anna. Damn it, baby, I'm sorry. So sorry.

"Scurto," he said. His voice was farther away. "Don't waste another one."

Anna.

"Say I love you!" he shouted to me from across the cemetery. "Say it!"

I stared hard at the tombstone. I pressed my palm against it. I bowed my head and wept.

86

For You, Baby

Entry 86.

May 8th 11:30 pm. In another life we would be husband and wife, holding hands on the runway. In another life we would roll in the hay so often we'd bust the bed frame. In another life we would play cornhole wearing matching husband and wifey t-shirts. In another life we would have a barefoot mountain wedding in the middle of spring. In another life we would be a family, unified love in the bliss of wilderness living. In another life I gave you my heart. In another life I would be yours and you would be mine.

87

The End

Entry 87.

May 9th, 12:01 am. One day you wake up not knowing that you lost everything the night before. You run down the halls checking every closet, every drawer, under every bed. But her things are gone and so is she. There is no rewind. No starting over with the person from the past. There is no closure. No final good-bye. Nothing but the very words you began with on a dating site so long ago:

"Hi, I'm Damon. I really like your pics. So cute. Is that your real name or you go by something else?"

"Nice to meet you, Damon. Thanks. Actually my name's Anna. I just like having a funny screen name."

"Anna. I like that. So wanna trade numbers?"

"Sure."

And that is how she disappears.

That is how she moves on.

Forever.

About the Author

Han M. Greenbarg has been in love with writing fiction since childhood. She is an avid coffee drinker, proud dog mom, and lover of country music and war movies. She achieves her biggest jolts of inspiration while being out in nature, and especially enjoys crafting parallel worlds and post-apocalyptic settings. This is her first standalone short novel.

You can connect with me on:

🌐 https://www.hanmgreenbarg.com

www.ingramcontent.com/pod-product-compliance
Lightning Source LLC
Chambersburg PA
CBHW030748110726
47900CB00008B/2502